BENEATH

Book One: Signal

—

A Science Fiction Novel

Cole Vane

CAINOTA
cainota.com

SIGNAL

Book One of the BENEATH trilogy

This is a work of fiction. Names, characters, organizations, places, events, and incidents are either products of the author's imagination or are used fictitiously. Any resemblance to actual persons, living or dead, or to real events, locales, or organizations, is entirely coincidental.

Published by Cainota Publishing
cainota.com
First edition: 2026

ISBN (ebook): 978-9916-4-3892-3
ISBN (paperback): 978-9916-4-3893-0
ISBN (hardcover): 978-9916-4-3894-7

This book was produced with the assistance of AI tools used as part of the author's writing and editorial process. All creative decisions, narrative content, and final text are the work of the author.

They were here before us. They shaped us.
And now — after millennia of patience — something has changed.

CONTENTS

ACT ONE

The Data

ONE

Noise

The survey had been logged, certified, and filed three days ago. Eighteen hours of sonar data from the Lofoten's run along the Mohns Ridge, reviewed by two of my colleagues, signed off by Professor Langvik, and uploaded to the institute's server with a timestamp and a green checkmark. Done. Verified. Closed.

I was reading it again at two in the morning.

This was not unusual. I kept a list on a yellow legal pad on my desk at home, going back eleven years, of every dataset I'd reviewed after it had already been cleared. The list was seventy-three pages long. Langvik, if he ever found out about it, would call it a pathology. He might be right. But in those seventy-three pages, filed in order by date and survey coordinates, I had found eleven things that other people had missed. Small things, mostly. A calibration drift that turned out to be a previously undocumented cold seep. A pattern of micro-tremors along a section of ridge that suggested fault geometry nobody had mapped. Things that mattered to almost no one except me and the small number of oceanographers who specialised in the deep-ridge seismic activity of the Norwegian Sea.

I am Dr. Mara Voss. I am thirty-eight years old. I have been right about eleven things that nobody wanted to hear, and wrong about nothing I've published, because I've published almost nothing. This is the trade I made, twelve years ago, without fully understanding I was making it.

I poured a second coffee and went back to the data.

The Lofoten is a research vessel operated by the Birkeland Institute of Marine Sciences in Tromsø, where I've worked since my postdoc. She's 73 metres, purpose-built for deep-survey work, with a hull-mounted multibeam sonar system and a towed array that can reach hadal depths. The survey run three days ago had been routine — a repeat pass of a section of the Mohns Ridge we grid every two years for seismic baseline data. We were looking for nothing in particular. We were building the record.

The data was not interesting.

Most data isn't. This is something they don't tell you when you start a career in marine geophysics — that the overwhelming majority of the ocean floor is exactly what you expect it to be. Rock. Sediment. The slow, pressurised dark. The anomalies are genuinely rare, which is why the people who spend their careers waiting for them are considered eccentric.

I had the recording open on three screens. The primary display showed the sonar sweep as a scrolling visualisation — depth rendered in false colour, the ridge rising and falling in shades of blue and green, geological time compressed into a strip of data three centimetres wide. On the second screen I had the raw acoustic files, displayed as waveforms. On the third I was running a spectral analysis programme I'd written myself five years ago, which filtered out the frequency ranges associated with the ship's engines, the ambient noise of the current, the biological scatter — whale clicks, shrimp, the low-frequency rumble of distant shipping traffic — and highlighted anything that remained.

At 03.17 in the morning, the third screen showed me something that shouldn't have been there.

* * *

It was not dramatic. I want to be precise about this, because in the weeks and months that followed, when I tried to describe what I saw and what I felt, people kept reaching for the word revelation. It was not a revelation. It was a number.

A sequence, to be exact. Embedded in what the survey system had logged as background noise at a depth of approximately 4,200 metres, directly below our survey track at 11.43 degrees East, 73.17 degrees North. A sequence of pressure pulses, low-frequency, outside the range of any biological source I was aware of, with an interval structure that was — and I ran the analysis four times before I wrote anything down — regular.

Not regular in the way geological processes are regular, where regularity means slow and approximate and shaped by forces that don't care about precision. Regular in the way a metronome is regular. Regular in the way a mathematical sequence is regular. The interval between the first and second pulse was 4.3 seconds. Between the second and third: 4.3 seconds. Between the second and third: 4.3 seconds. Between each of the six: 4.3 seconds. Then a pause of 8.6 seconds — exactly double — and then the sequence again. Six pulses. Pause. Six pulses.

I sat with it for a long time before I touched anything.

I had found anomalous readings before. That was, in a real sense, my speciality. In 2017 I'd found a temperature gradient in deep-ridge sediment core data that turned out to be a misrecorded instrument malfunction. In 2019 I'd found an acoustic signature in a survey off Bear Island that I was convinced for three weeks was a previously undocumented hydrothermal vent system, and which turned out, on follow-up survey, to be a crashed Soviet satellite from 1984. I knew what it felt like to find something that looked like something and turned out to be nothing. I knew the particular flavour of premature certainty.

This was different. The difference was in the precision. Geological processes don't produce 4.3-second intervals. They produce approximations, shaped by variable pressures and temperatures and the inherent messiness of the physical world. Biological sources don't maintain that kind of regularity either — whale song, the closest analogue, has temporal structure but not mathematical interval structure of this kind. What I was looking at was precise in a way that suggested intention.

I did not let myself think the word that goes with intention. Not yet. Instead I ran the analysis again, and then once more, using different filter parameters. The sequence was present in all three runs. I isolated the frequency range and checked it against the background noise floor — the sequence was distinct, not an artifact of the filtering. I checked the ship's log for the time window in question: no mechanical activity, no equipment tests, no known sources of low-frequency acoustic emission.

It was 03.49. I had been looking at it for thirty-two minutes.

I made a copy to my personal drive. Then I closed the analysis programme, shut down the secondary screens, and put my coffee mug in the small galley sink. I stood at the porthole for a moment. Outside, the Norwegian Sea was black and still, the sky beginning to show the first grey suggestion of the short northern summer night giving way. Below us, 3,100 metres of cold water.

I went back to my desk and started writing notes.

* * *

I should explain the vessel, and my situation on it.

Research cruises at Birkeland run on a rotation system. The Lofoten is at sea for roughly nine months of the year, with a crew of twelve and a rotating scientific staff of up to eight. I had been on this particular cruise for eighteen days. We were eleven days from return to Tromsø. My role was lead geophysicist for the seismic survey programme, which meant I had oversight of the sonar operations, the data collection protocols, and the preliminary analysis reports that went to Langvik at the end of each week.

It was a good position. It was the best position I was likely to occupy for some time, given my publication record. I was aware of both of these things.

I had one colleague on board who worked in my area: Dr. Petter Halvorsen, a sedimentologist five years my junior who published regularly, got along well with Langvik, and approached the deep sea with the professional enthusiasm of a man who had not yet spent twelve years being told his readings were instrument error. We shared the data deck — a long, low room full of monitors and workstations below the main lab — but kept different hours. He was morning. I was late night. We had reached an unspoken arrangement whereby the data deck was mine from eleven pm to whenever he arrived, which was usually around seven.

I had three hours before Halvorsen arrived. I used them.

What I did in those three hours was not look at the sequence again. I already knew what was there. What I did was work backwards through the recording, looking for anything I might have missed — any signal, any artifact, any precursor to the sequence that might explain it. I found nothing. The sequence appeared out of the background noise without warning and disappeared the same way. Six pulses, the doubled pause, six more pulses. Total duration: 82.8 seconds. And then nothing.

I also ran a check against every known acoustic source in the region. Shipping traffic: the nearest vessel at the time of the recording had been a Norwegian coast guard patrol boat, 140 kilometres west, and I could see its signature in the data as a faint continuous rumble in an entirely different frequency range. Seismic activity: the ridge had been quiet that night, a baseline micro-tremor profile with nothing anomalous. Military activity: I had no access to that data and no way to check it, which I noted.

At 06.20, I locked my personal drive in the drawer under my workstation and went to breakfast.

* * *

The mess on the Lofoten holds twelve people comfortably. At 06.20 it held three: the watch officer, a deck hand named Torben who ate with methodical speed and never spoke before eight, and me. I ate porridge and looked at the sea through the wide mess windows.

The Norwegian Sea in June is not beautiful in any simple way. It is vast and grey and cold and it has the quality, on clear mornings like this one, of being extremely indifferent to your presence in it. I had spent a significant portion of my adult life on or in it, and I had never stopped finding it mildly hostile in the way that large indifferent things are mildly hostile: not threatening, just unconcerned.

Below us, at this moment: 1,200 metres of water. Below that, the Mohns Ridge, a section of the Mid-Arctic spreading centre, running roughly east-northeast for six hundred kilometres. Below the ridge: the upper mantle of the earth, where everything is heat and pressure and geological time.

And, at 4,200 metres, in the background noise of the ocean, a sequence that shouldn't exist.

I finished my porridge.

What I was not doing, in those hours between finding the sequence and breakfast, was panicking. I want to be clear about this because it seems, in retrospect, like it should be the most natural response to what I'd found. But panic requires a degree of certainty that I didn't have. What I had was a signal I couldn't explain. That was not the same thing as knowing what the signal was.

I had spent twelve years in a field that dismissed anomalous readings as instrument error. I had spent twelve years being the person who said: wait, look at this again. I had been right, eleven times, about small things. And I had been not-wrong but also not-proven about the larger category of anomaly I had been tracking for the past three years — the deep low-frequency readings in the hadal zones of the Norwegian Sea and Greenland Basin that I believed, and had failed to convince anyone else, were worth systematic study.

The sequence I'd found that morning could be many things. It could be a previously undocumented natural source. It could be military. It could be an artifact I hadn't identified yet. I was not, at 06.20 in the mess of the RV Lofoten, prepared to tell myself it was something else.

But I had made a copy to my personal drive. And I had not noted it in the preliminary analysis report that would go to Langvik at the end of the week.

These were not accidental omissions.

* * *

Halvorsen arrived at the data deck at 07.15, earlier than usual. He had the slightly compressed energy of a man who had an idea overnight and was eager to get to it. He glanced at my screen — I had the standard display up, nothing unusual — and said good morning, and sat down at his own workstation.

I stayed for another forty minutes, finishing a report on the microtremor baseline data, before I went to my cabin and slept for four hours.

When I woke up, I wrote four pages of notes by hand in a journal I kept locked in my cabin. Then I lay on my bunk and looked at the ceiling and thought about the sequence for another hour.

I thought about the frequency range. About the interval structure. About the location: not a random point in open water, but directly over the deepest accessible section of the ridge, at a depth consistent with the lower hadal zone.

I thought: I need to go back.

I thought: I need more data.

I thought: if I tell anyone what I found, it will be dismissed before I have more data, and I will spend the next year trying to get back to that location with the standing of a researcher who reported anomalous readings and turned out to be wrong.

I thought: I have been here before. Not exactly here. But close enough.

I lay there for a while longer. Outside my porthole the sea moved the way it moves — slow and grey and comprehensive — and the Lofoten's engines ran at their standard 220 rpm and the world was entirely normal, entirely ordinary, and somewhere below us, 4,200 metres down, there was a thing I had found and no one else knew about.

I got up. I went back to the data deck. I started writing the application for a research extension.

TWO

The Rig

The briefing was conducted in a windowless conference room on the fourth floor of the Naval Operations Centre in Suitland, Maryland, at 09.00 on a Tuesday morning in June. Present were Commander Eli Reyes, two intelligence analysts he'd worked with before and trusted at different levels, a representative from Naval Sea Systems Command whose name Reyes immediately forgot, and a Deputy Director from the Office of Naval Intelligence whose name he already knew and would have preferred not to.

The Deputy Director's name was Harlow. She had been at ONI for eleven years and had a particular gift for the kind of institutional brevity that sounded like confidence but was mostly the product of not wanting to be in the room any longer than necessary. She opened the briefing at 09.02.

"The NordDepth rig Aurora Seven went dark on June 3rd at 22.47 local time," she said. "Twenty-four crew. Last confirmed contact was a routine check-in at 21.00. No distress call. No debris field. No wreckage of any kind located in the forty-eight hours since."

She clicked to the next slide. It showed a map of the Norwegian Sea, a red marker at approximately 73.17 degrees North, 11.43 degrees East, and a radius circle indicating the search area.

"The rig was operating at a depth of 3,100 metres. The Norwegian Coast Guard has been coordinating a search and rescue operation since June 4th, in collaboration with NordDepth corporate. As of this morning, that operation has found nothing. No survival pods. No personal flotation devices. No oil slick. No acoustic signature consistent with structural failure."

Reyes looked at the map. He had a habit in briefings of not writing anything down until he'd asked at least three questions, because the first three questions almost always revealed what wasn't in the slide deck. He asked the first one now.

"What was the weather?"

Harlow glanced at the analyst to her left. The analyst said: "Sea state two at last contact, rising to three by midnight. Winds eight to twelve knots."

"So not weather."

"No."

Reyes nodded. He asked the second question. "What does the seabed look like at that location?"

A longer pause. The Naval Sea Systems Command representative, who had not spoken yet and whose name Reyes still didn't know, said: "Deep-ridge terrain. Part of the Jan Mayen Ridge system. Significant topographic variation. Not ideal for visual survey."

"But not impossible."

"Not impossible. Just slow."

Reyes asked the third question. "What's the working theory?"

Harlow said: "Catastrophic structural failure. Deep implosion."

Reyes said: "Twenty-four people and no debris."

Harlow said: "That's correct."

There was a silence in the room. Reyes had been in enough briefings to recognise the particular quality of a silence that meant: we know it doesn't hold up; we're telling you anyway.

* * *

He had read the preliminary incident report on the flight from Norfolk that morning, and he had read it the way he read all incident reports — looking not at what was there but at the shape of what wasn't. The shape here was very clear: the official working theory required the Aurora Seven to have imploded so completely and so cleanly that it left no surface trace whatsoever. This was, in principle, possible. A deep implosion at 3,100 metres, under the right conditions, could produce a debris field that sank straight down rather than dispersing laterally.

You'd lose the oil slick. You might lose the larger structural sections if they hit the seafloor in a confined canyon.

You would not lose the survival pods.

Every offshore rig of Aurora Seven's class carried four self-deploying survival pods, each rated for six occupants, each fitted with its own emergency beacon and designed to separate automatically from the structure if the hull integrity sensors detected a catastrophic event. The beacons were hardened against pressure failure. The pods themselves were designed to float free of any depth down to 4,000 metres.

None of them had deployed. None of them had been found. The beacons were silent.

An implosion fast enough to prevent pod deployment would have needed to happen in less than 0.3 seconds. That was theoretically within the range of catastrophic hull failure under extreme pressure differential, but it required a failure mode that had never been observed on a rig of this type, in a location with no geological activity recorded in the 72 hours preceding the loss.

Reyes had noted all of this in the margin of his copy of the report, in his compact, vertical handwriting. He had also noted two other things.

One: the Aurora Seven had gone dark without sending a distress signal. Not a partial signal, not a corrupted signal — no signal at all. The communications system used a redundant architecture with three independent transmitters. For all three to fail simultaneously, in the fraction of a second before an implosion, was mathematically possible. It was not, in Reyes's estimation, probable.

Two: the rig had been operating in an area that had seen two other deep-survey operations in the preceding eighteen months, both of which had reported anomalous sonar returns that had been attributed to geological interference. He had found this in a footnote. Nobody had thought it worth including in the main text.

* * *

After the briefing, Harlow asked him to stay behind. The others filed out. She waited until the door was closed.

"You're going to tell me it isn't an implosion," she said.

"I'm going to tell you I'd like to see the full sensor logs from the 72 hours before loss."

"We have them."

"I'd also like the full search and rescue operation records, including the Norwegian Coast Guard's acoustic survey data." He paused. "And the anomalous sonar returns from the two previous operations. The ones in the footnote."

Harlow looked at him for a moment. She had the expression of someone who had been expecting a specific kind of problem and had just confirmed it. "This is going to be a visibility issue," she said. "NordDepth is a Norwegian company with significant US interests. Their government is already making inquiries at the diplomatic level. We don't want this to look like —"

"I understand the visibility concern," Reyes said. "What I'd like to avoid is going to the Norwegian Sea and finding something that should have been in the main text of the briefing document."

Another pause. Harlow had a habit of pausing in a way that was also a form of assessment — she was deciding, each time, how much to acknowledge. She said: "You'll operate under a cover designation. Safety audit, requested by NordDepth's insurance consortium. You'll have access to NordDepth facilities and personnel as required. The Norwegians are cooperating."

"And my actual brief?"

"Find out what happened to Aurora Seven. If there's a hull somewhere on that seafloor, locate it. If there are survivors" — she paused again, briefly — "locate them."

"And if it's not an implosion?"

She picked up her folder. "Then you'll tell me what it is instead."

* * *

Commander Eli Reyes was forty-five years old and had spent twenty-two of those years in the United States Navy, the last twelve in deep-sea operations. He was lean, dark-haired going grey at the temples, and possessed of the particular stillness of people who had spent a significant portion of their careers in confined spaces where unnecessary movement was a liability. His colleagues described him as methodical.

His CO, a Vice Admiral named Chen who had worked with him twice before, described him in evaluation reports as relentlessly literal, which was not quite a compliment and not quite the opposite.

He had a gift for the anomaly. Not the dramatic anomaly — not the crisis that announced itself and demanded immediate response. The quiet anomaly. The footnote. The number that was slightly wrong in a way that only mattered if you were looking at it from exactly the right angle. He had found, in his career: a navigation discrepancy in a submarine exercise that turned out to indicate a previously unmapped seamount in the Philippine Sea. A maintenance schedule inconsistency that had preceded, by eleven days, a near-catastrophic mechanical failure in a deep-survey vessel operating off Greenland. A pattern of sonar interference that had led, eventually, to the identification of a foreign acoustic monitoring installation in the North Atlantic.

He did not consider this a talent. He considered it a practice. The anomaly was always there if you looked for it. Most people didn't look. Reyes looked as a matter of professional habit, the way some people checked the exits when they entered a room.

He did not, as a rule, share this practice with people who hadn't asked about it. There was a version of his career that would have been considerably smoother if he'd reported to his superiors with greater selectivity — if he'd learned to distinguish between the anomalies that mattered and the ones that were going to turn out to be instrument error, Soviet satellites, geological noise. He hadn't learned to make that distinction, because he hadn't found a reliable method. The only way to know which kind of anomaly you were looking at was to look at it until you knew.

This was, among other things, why he was being sent to the Norwegian Sea to conduct what was officially a safety audit.

* * *

On the flight back to Norfolk he read the full sensor logs from Aurora Seven's last 72 hours. The data was dense and most of it was routine — drilling operations, station-keeping adjustments, weather monitoring, routine equipment checks logged at four-hour intervals. He read all of it.

Near the end of the second hour of reading, he found the footnote's footnote.

In Aurora Seven's automated environmental monitoring log — a subsystem that ran continuously in the background, recording ambient conditions around the rig — there was a series of entries beginning approximately 58 hours before loss. They were brief. They read:

Low-frequency acoustic anomaly detected. Source unknown. Duration: 83 seconds. Intensity: below alert threshold. Classification: background noise.

Low-frequency acoustic anomaly detected. Source unknown. Duration: 37 seconds. Intensity: below alert threshold. Classification: background noise.

Low-frequency acoustic anomaly detected. Source unknown. Duration: 83 seconds. Intensity: below alert threshold. Classification: background noise.

There were six entries total, spanning 58 hours. The first and third and fifth were 83 seconds. The second and fourth and sixth were 37 seconds. Alternating. Regular.

The system had logged them as background noise and flagged none of them for human review. In the standard operations report, they didn't appear at all.

Reyes looked at the alternating durations for a long time. Eighty-three seconds and thirty-seven seconds. He wrote in the margin: Two transmission types. Alternating. Internal interval ratio 2:1. Consistent. Not random.

He wrote below that: Source unknown.

He looked out the window. Thirty-five thousand feet below, the Atlantic was grey and comprehensive and contained, in its depths, approximately one-third of the world's ocean water and a number of things that were not yet known.

He closed the folder. He would read it again when he landed. He would read it several more times after that.

The flight attendant asked if he wanted anything. He said coffee, black, and thank you.

He thought about the alternating durations for the rest of the flight.

THREE

Twelve Years

I presented the anomaly to Professor Langvik on the first Monday after we returned to Tromsø. I had spent the intervening eleven days on the return leg of the cruise preparing a full analysis, which I then spent two more days refining at my desk in the institute before requesting the meeting. I wanted to be certain. I also wanted to be certain that I was certain, which is a different thing and took longer.

The analysis ran to forty-one pages including appendices. I had printed it and put it in a folder with a cover page. I was aware, as I carried it down the corridor to Langvik's office, that forty-one pages was perhaps a great deal of paper for a conversation that might last twenty minutes. I had decided to bring it anyway. You don't present an anomaly of this kind with a summary.

Langvik's office was on the second floor of the institute's main building, overlooking the harbour. He had been department head for nine years. He was sixty-one, silver-haired, and gave the impression of a man who had once been very interested in deep-sea geomorphology and had, gradually and without drama, transferred that interest to the administration of people who were still interested in it. He was not unkind. He was not obstructionist. He was, in the most specific and technical sense of the phrase, not the right person to show this to — and he was the only person I could show it to, because he was my department head and this was my institute and those were the rules.

He was on a call when I arrived. His assistant waved me to the chair outside his door. I sat for fourteen minutes, the folder on my lap, and looked at the harbour.

* * *

The meeting lasted twenty-three minutes. I know this because I checked my watch when I sat down and again when I left.

I walked Langvik through the analysis in order: the detection parameters, the filtering methodology, the raw waveform data, the spectral analysis, the interval structure of the sequence. He listened. He had reading glasses that he put on to look at the printed waveforms and then took off again when I was talking. He asked three questions. The first was whether I had checked the data against the ship's own low-frequency emission profile — I had, and had included the comparison in appendix B. The second was whether the towed array had been recently calibrated — it had, twelve days before the survey, and I had included the calibration logs in appendix C. The third was whether I had considered the possibility of biological source.

I had expected this question. I had three pages on it. I explained that the frequency range of the sequence fell below the lowest known limit of biological acoustic production in the Norwegian Sea, that the interval regularity was inconsistent with any known biological rhythm, and that the directional analysis placed the source directly below the survey track at a depth consistent with the lower hadal zone, where biological acoustic activity of any kind was vanishingly rare.

Langvik nodded. He looked at the waveform printout for a moment. Then he said: "Mara, I think this is instrument error."

I did not say anything for a moment. Then I said: "I've accounted for every possible source of instrument error in appendix A. The analysis uses three independent filtering methods, all of which produce the same result."

"The towed array has been flagging false positives in the low-frequency range since the February refit," he said. "There's a known resonance issue. Maintenance has a ticket open on it."

"The calibration log from twelve days before the survey shows no anomalous resonance in the relevant frequency range," I said. "It's in appendix C."

"Calibration tests don't always catch intermittent resonance." He said this gently. He had the manner, which I had encountered before in this office, of a person delivering a verdict they considered closed while appearing to engage with the evidence. "I'll ask maintenance to take another look at the array before the next cruise. If the issue persists, we'll know to discount readings in this range."

I said: "The interval structure is consistent across six separate readings over a period of approximately ninety seconds. Instrument resonance doesn't produce mathematically regular intervals."

He looked at me. He had kind eyes, Langvik. I have always thought this, and I have always found it one of the more frustrating things about him. "Mara," he said. "You've been finding things in the background noise of deep-survey data for as long as I've known you. Most of them have turned out to be explicable. This one will too. Write it up as an anomaly note, flag it for follow-up, and move on to the March dataset. We're already behind on the ridge survey analysis and the stakeholder report is due in three weeks."

I picked up my folder. I said: "I'd like to request a research extension to conduct a follow-up survey at the same coordinates."

He had clearly not expected this. He paused, and for a moment his expression shifted into something more attentive, the way it did when an administrative problem arrived that required actual thought. "On what budget line?"

"My discretionary research allocation. I still have eleven thousand kroner unspent from last quarter."

Another pause. "That's not enough to extend the Lofoten's schedule."

"I'm not asking to extend the schedule. I'm asking for four additional survey days at the end of the current cruise deployment window. The Lofoten returns to the same general area in August for the Bear Island baseline run. I'm asking to add a four-day deviation to the return leg."

Langvik looked at the harbour. A small cargo vessel was moving out of the far berth, slow and purposeful. He said: "Four days of additional operations costs considerably more than eleven thousand kroner."

"I'm prepared to cover the difference from my personal research fund," I said. "I have funds remaining from the ERC grant."

He turned back to look at me. I held his gaze. He said: "I'll consider it," which meant he was going to approve it and didn't want to say so in the room.

I thanked him and left.

* * *

In the corridor outside his office, I stopped for a moment and looked at the fire evacuation map on the wall. It was old enough that one of the exits had been labelled in a font that no longer existed on any of the institute's computers. I had looked at this map many times over twelve years. I had never actually needed to evacuate.

Twelve years. I counted from my first posting to Birkeland as a post-doctoral researcher, when I was twenty-six and had recently defended a thesis on seismic signatures of deep-ridge hydrothermal circulation that my committee had described, with careful calibration, as thorough. I had arrived with the reasonable expectation of a scientific career in which I found things, published papers about them, and was taken seriously. Two of these three had occurred, in modified form. I had found things. I had taken myself seriously. The publishing had proved more difficult.

It was not that my findings were wrong. The problem was structural and could be stated plainly: I found things in data that other people had already reviewed and certified and moved on from, which meant that every finding required me to argue, implicitly, that the previous reviewers had missed something. This was not a position from which it was easy to publish. Reviewers did not enjoy the implication. Editors appreciated caution. And Langvik, who signed off on all external submissions from the department, had a specific and consistent concern about what he called overreach — the gap between what the data showed and what the researcher claimed it showed.

* * *

The first time I had been in Langvik's office for a conversation of this kind, I was twenty-nine. I had found a pattern of micro-tremors in baseline survey data from the Greenland Basin — a pattern that, if you filtered the data correctly, suggested a previously unmapped fault structure running along the eastern wall of the basin at approximately 2,800 metres depth. I had a forty-page analysis then too. Langvik had listened politely, asked two questions, and suggested that the pattern was likely the result of instrument drift compounding over the survey period.

I had gone back to the data. I had ruled out instrument drift. I had written a revised analysis demonstrating this. I had brought it back to Langvik. He had listened again, more briefly, and suggested that before taking it further I should have the analysis independently reviewed by someone with expertise in fault geometry.

I had found someone with expertise in fault geometry. He was a Norwegian-American academic named Brøgger who was on the faculty at the University of Bergen and had published extensively on North Atlantic fault systems. He had looked at my analysis and said it was interesting and asked if I had considered instrument drift. I said I had ruled it out. He said that in his experience these things had a way of turning up when you least expected them.

I had not published that paper. The fault structure remains unmapped.

Three years later, a survey conducted by a German research consortium in the same area had found a fault structure consistent with what I had described, at a depth of approximately 2,850 metres. It was treated as a new discovery. The lead researcher was a man named Fischer who had never read my analysis because I had never published it, and who received a commendation from the German Marine Research Association for the finding. I read about it in a journal abstract on a Tuesday morning and then went for a very long walk along the waterfront and came back and made coffee and did not mention it to anyone.

That was the first time. There had been others.

* * *

I want to be precise about what those twelve years were and were not.

They were not a period of suppression. Nobody told me not to pursue my research. Nobody blocked my access to data. Langvik had never been actively obstructive — he had, on three occasions, approved extensions and additional survey time that he could reasonably have denied. The institute had a functional library and decent computing resources and colleagues who were, for the most part, professionally courteous.

They were not a period of bitterness, either, at least not in the productive sense that bitterness sometimes gives people energy. I had looked at bitterness, in the years after the Greenland Basin paper and the Fischer finding and the other occasions that followed, and decided against it. Bitterness is inaccurate. It requires you to believe that what happened to you was unjust, and I was not certain it was. What happened to me was that I kept finding things in data that other people had reviewed and cleared, I kept being unable to convince those people that I was right, and the findings kept turning out, on the rare occasions when they could be independently verified, to be correct. This was not injustice. It was a sequence of events with a clear causal structure that I had chosen to continue participating in.

What those twelve years were, exactly, was this: a long time to be right without being believed.

I had been precise about this for the full twelve years, and I intended to continue being precise about it, because the alternative — the version where I allowed the weight of it to accrue into something less controlled — would not help me get back to those coordinates, 73.17 North and 11.43 East, at 4,200 metres depth, to find out what was there.

* * *

Langvik approved the extension four days later, by email, while I was in the middle of reviewing the March dataset. He had approved it with two conditions: that I stayed within the allocated budget line, and that I filed a standard anomaly report with the institute's data registry before the follow-up survey, so that if the extension produced null results there would be a formal record that the anomaly had been investigated and closed.

He framed this as a procedural requirement. It was also, I understood, a way of ensuring that if I found nothing, the finding would be officially documented as nothing. Filed. Certified. Closed.

I filed the anomaly report the same afternoon. In the description field, under the heading Nature of anomaly, I wrote: Low-frequency acoustic sequence detected in deep-survey background noise at 73.17°N, 11.43°E, depth approximately 4,200m. Interval structure consistent and non-random. Source unknown. Follow-up survey scheduled.

In the field marked Probable cause, I left a single word: Unknown.

The form had a dropdown menu for that field. The options were: instrument error, biological source, geological source, human activity, and unknown. I selected unknown. It was the first time I had used that option in twelve years. All my previous anomaly reports said instrument error, because Langvik reviewed them and that was what he preferred.

This one was different.

I sent the report, closed my computer, and put on my coat. It was late enough in the day that most of the building had emptied. I walked down to the harbour and stood for a while at the edge of the water, looking north. The sky was that particular June blue that doesn't quite darken even at midnight, a shade that has no name in any language I know but that I associate completely and only with Tromsø and with the specific feeling of being very far north and very far from being finished.

The Lofoten was at berth two hundred metres away. She would go out again in six weeks, on the Bear Island baseline run. I had four additional days on the return leg, and eleven thousand kroner of my own research budget, and a forty-one-page analysis that one person had read and dismissed, and a sequence of pressure pulses at 4,200 metres that I had run through every filter I had and could not explain.

I had been here before. Not exactly here. But close enough that I knew what came next.

You go back. You get more data. You find out what it is.

I walked home. I had dinner. I called Yuna, who picked up on the second ring and immediately said: "You found something, didn't you? You have the voice."

I said: "What voice?"

She said: "The one where you're being very calm about something that you're not calm about at all."

I said: "I'm going to tell you about it soon. Not yet."

She said: "Okay." A pause. Then: "Is it a big one?"

I looked at the wall of my kitchen for a moment. "I don't know yet," I said. Which was true. I didn't know. I had a sequence of 83-second pulses at 4,200 metres and a Langvik who had said instrument error and a research extension I had partially funded with my own money, and somewhere out there, below the Norwegian Sea, there was something I had found and could not explain.

I said: "I'll call you when I know more."
I hung up. I did the dishes. I went to bed.
I did not sleep for a very long time.

FOUR

Aurora Seven

Bergen received him in the middle of a grey morning, low cloud sitting on the seven mountains like a lid, the harbour busy with the particular purposeful traffic of a working port. Reyes took a taxi from the airport directly to the NordDepth regional operations centre on Bryggen, a modern glass-and-steel building inserted with evident care into a row of old Hanseatic warehouses, close enough to the water that he could smell it through the taxi window.

He had been in Bergen once before, twelve years ago, for a joint NATO exercise involving Norwegian coastal defence assets. He remembered it as a city that took its geography seriously — the mountains on three sides, the fjord opening to the west, the sense of being held in a particular place by the landscape rather than simply occupying it. It had not changed in any way he could identify. He supposed cities that were held in place by mountains didn't change quickly.

The NordDepth building had a security desk staffed by a man in his thirties who checked Reyes's credentials with the focused neutrality of someone trained to be neither welcoming nor suspicious. Reyes handed over his cover identification — Commander Eli Reyes, US Navy, representing the International Maritime Safety Consortium on behalf of Aurora Seven's insurers — and waited while it was verified. The man made a call. After two minutes he handed back the documents and said, in excellent English, that Mr. Moen was expecting him and that someone would be down shortly.

Someone was down in four minutes. She was a woman in her forties named Ingrid Berge, who identified herself as NordDepth's Director of Offshore Operations and walked with the brisk economy of someone whose default speed was faster than the situation required. She shook his hand, said she hoped his flight had been acceptable, and led him to a lift without waiting to find out.

"Mr. Moen has cleared his morning," she said, as they rose. "He asked me to tell you that NordDepth's full cooperation is unconditional. Whatever you need."

Reyes said: "I appreciate that."

"He also asked me to tell you" — a brief pause, the kind that precedes something that has been carefully phrased — "that Aurora Seven's crew had an average tenure with the company of seven years. Several of them were on their fourth or fifth offshore rotation. They were not strangers."

Reyes looked at her. She was looking at the lift doors. He said: "I understand."

"He wants you to know that," she said. "Before you meet him."

The lift opened. She led him down a corridor with floor-to-ceiling windows looking out over the harbour. Below, a red cargo vessel was easing away from the commercial quay, its wake spreading in a thin white V. Reyes watched it for a moment as he walked.

* * *

Aldric Moen was fifty-seven years old and looked it in the way that people who have spent their careers in demanding industries look it — not deteriorated, exactly, but fully occupied, the way a building that has been in continuous use develops a specific kind of worn authority. He was broad across the shoulders, silver-haired, and when he stood to greet Reyes he did so with the unhurried deliberateness of a large man who had learned early that unhurried and deliberate conveyed something that hurried and demonstrative did not.

His office was corner-facing, harbour on two sides. On the desk: two monitors, a coffee press, a framed photograph turned away from visitors that Reyes noted without looking at. On the wall behind him: a topographic map of the Norwegian Sea, annotated in marker. Reyes recognised the Aurora Seven site immediately — there was a circled point on the map, a date written beside it in small, careful numbers, and below the date a line that connected it to a note in the margin that Reyes could not read from across the room.

Moen offered coffee. Reyes accepted. They sat.

"I'll save us both time," Moen said. His English was precise, nearly accent-free, the product of a decade at an international company. "I know you're not here on behalf of the insurance consortium. The consortium sent their own people two weeks ago and closed their preliminary assessment. You're a Navy officer conducting an investigation that someone has decided shouldn't look like one."

Reyes said: "I'm not going to confirm or deny the institutional context of my investigation."

"I know," Moen said. "I'm not asking you to. I'm telling you that I know, because I want you to know that I'm cooperating with the actual investigation and not the cover story. I find cover stories slow things down."

He said this without heat. It was a statement of professional preference, not an accusation. Reyes adjusted his estimate of the man slightly upward.

"Then I'll tell you what I need," Reyes said. "The full operational record for Aurora Seven's final deployment. Drilling logs, environmental monitoring data, communications logs, crew schedules. And the maintenance records from the sixty days before the loss."

"You have them," Moen said. "Ingrid will give you access to our secure documentation server before you leave the building." He paused. "Is there something specific you're looking for?"

"I'll know it when I find it."

Moen looked at him for a moment, and something crossed his face that Reyes couldn't immediately categorise — not suspicion, not evasion. Something closer to recognition. "That's not a reassuring answer," he said.

"It's the honest one."

Another pause. Moen poured himself coffee with the careful attention of a man using a small action to manage a large feeling. He said: "Twenty-four people. I've spoken to all of their families. There are forty-one children between them." He set the coffee press down. "I know what the working theory is. I know why it doesn't hold up. I have my own engineering team's analysis, which reaches conclusions I was told, by people above my pay grade, to treat as preliminary." He looked at the harbour. "I want to know what happened to my crew."

Reyes said: "So do I."

They looked at each other. Outside, Bergen went about its grey morning, indifferent to both of them.

* * *

The documentation server was in a secure workroom on the third floor, accessible by keycard, staffed by a young data analyst named Kristoffer who had been assigned to assist Reyes and who had the expression of someone who had been told to be helpful without being told how much.

Reyes spent three hours in that room.

He worked through the documentation in the same order he always used: structural first, operational second, environmental third. The structural logs told him nothing he didn't already know — Aurora Seven was a fourth-generation semi-submersible rig, Class 4 deepwater, maintained to standard, last full inspection fourteen months before the loss, no outstanding structural deficiencies flagged. The operational logs were dense and unremarkable: drilling activity, weather adjustments, routine equipment cycles, a minor hydraulic issue in the third-deck crane that had been logged and repaired six weeks before the loss.

The environmental monitoring logs were where he slowed down.

He had expected to find the six anomaly entries he'd already seen in the preliminary data — the alternating 83-second and 37-second low-frequency detections in the 58 hours before loss. They were there. But in the full environmental log, unfiltered and complete, there was more.

Forty-three days before the loss, the environmental monitoring system had logged a single low-frequency detection. Duration: 83 seconds. Source unknown. Below alert threshold. Classified as background noise.

Thirty-one days before the loss: another. Duration: 83 seconds. Same classification.

Twenty-two days before: 37 seconds.

Fourteen days before: 83 seconds.

Nine days before: 37 seconds.

Then, beginning 58 hours before loss: the six entries he already had, alternating, regular, building in frequency.

He sat with this for a while. In the preliminary data he'd been given — the data that had made it into the incident report — only the final six entries appeared. The earlier detections, spread across forty-three days, had been filtered out of the operational summary at some point in the reporting chain. Not suppressed, he thought. Just below the threshold of significance that someone had set. Background noise, filed, ignored.

He counted the entries. Eleven total. The interval between them was not perfectly regular — the early detections were weeks apart, the later ones days apart, the final six spread over 58 hours. But the pattern was clear if you were looking for it: the frequency was increasing. Whatever had been producing these signals had been producing them, at low intensity, for over a month before the rig went dark. And in the final days, it had been producing them more often.

Kristoffer, at his own workstation on the other side of the room, was doing something with a spreadsheet. Reyes looked at him for a moment.

"The environmental monitoring system," Reyes said. "Does it archive raw waveform data, or just the detection summaries?"

Kristoffer looked up. "Raw waveform data for any detection above the alert threshold. Below the threshold, it just logs the summary entry."

"All eleven of these entries are below threshold."

"Yes." Kristoffer paused. "There's no raw data for below-threshold detections. The system doesn't keep it."

Reyes nodded slowly. He looked back at the log. Eleven entries. No raw waveform data. The shape of the thing — its duration, its regularity, its increasing frequency — but not the thing itself.

He made copies of the complete environmental log, all forty-three days, including the early detections that had not made it into the incident report. He put the copies on his encrypted drive.

He did not ask Kristoffer about the early detections. He did not mention what he'd found to Ingrid Berge when she checked on him at noon. When Moen met him at the lift on his way out and asked if he had found what he was looking for, Reyes said he had found a great deal of useful material and that he would be in touch.

Moen held the lift door for a moment. He said: "The anomalous sonar returns. From the two operations in the area before ours." He said it quietly, not looking at Reyes. "I read about them in the incident report footnote. I had our environmental team cross-reference them against our own detection logs."

Reyes said: "And?"

Moen let the lift door go. He said: "The frequency range was consistent." He paused. "I don't know what that means. I thought you might."

Reyes said: "Not yet."

He stepped into the lift. Moen stayed in the corridor, one hand still resting on the door frame, looking at the middle distance in the way of a man who has been running a calculation for several weeks and has arrived at a result he does not know what to do with.

The lift doors closed.

* * *

He ate lunch at a small place near the quay — fish soup, bread, coffee — and went through his notes. The complete environmental log was open on his laptop. He had marked the eleven entries in red and drawn a timeline down the margin: 43 days, 31, 22, 14, 9, then the final six compressed into 58 hours.

He thought about what Moen had said: the frequency range was consistent.

Consistent with the two previous operations in the area. Which meant whatever was producing these signals had been there before Aurora Seven. Had been there, producing signals, and had been logged and filtered and classified as background noise across multiple independent survey operations, possibly for years.

He looked at the timeline. Forty-three days before the rig went dark. Then thirty-one. Twenty-two. Fourteen. Nine. Then six detections in the final two and a half days.

The gap between the first detection and the loss was forty-three days. In those forty-three days, the detections had come more and more frequently. He didn't know what that meant. He knew what it looked like.

It looked like something paying closer and closer attention.

He closed the laptop. He drank his coffee. He looked at the harbour, at the grey water and the mountains behind the city and the particular quality of light that came off the Norwegian Sea in summer — bright but remote, as though the sun had delegated illumination to something else.

He had what he needed for now. He would go back to the documentation server tomorrow for the communications logs and the crew schedules. He would request the raw acoustic data from the two earlier survey operations in the area.

And then he would track down whichever research vessels had run deep-survey operations in that area recently, because he had a feeling — not yet a conclusion, just a feeling — that whoever had been working those coordinates had found something they were also not quite sure what to do with.

He left enough kroner on the table to cover the bill and walked back towards the hotel.

Bergen closed around him as he walked — the narrow streets behind the Bryggen, the old wooden buildings leaning slightly toward each other overhead, the smell of the sea underlying everything. It was the kind of city that had existed in essentially the same relationship to the sea for a very long time, and that wore this fact as a specific kind of composure. Unremarkable, in the sense that things which have endured long enough stop requiring remark.

Reyes walked through it and thought about a rig that had gone dark without a trace, and a man in a corner office who had forty-one children to account for, and eleven entries in an environmental log that no one had thought significant enough to flag.

He thought: someone looked at this data and saw background noise.

He thought: I am not sure they were wrong to, given what they knew.

He thought: the question is what they didn't know.

He walked until he reached the hotel. He went up to his room. He opened the documentation files again and started at the beginning.

FIVE

The Second Look

There are things you can tell a research team and things you cannot. You cannot tell them that you believe you've found an anomaly of unknown origin in a stretch of deep water that the institute's department head has already classified as instrument error, that you've funded part of the follow-up survey with your own money, and that you've specifically requested this deviation from the Bear Island baseline run without telling anyone why. This information, delivered before the survey begins, would produce a certain kind of attention from your colleagues that would be worse than useless — more interested than you need, more sceptical than the data warrants, and impossible to manage while also trying to run the survey itself.

What you can tell them is that you identified a potential seismic anomaly on the previous run that merits a follow-up pass for baseline comparison, and that you've secured four additional survey days to do it properly. This is true. It is also incomplete. I had discovered, over twelve years, that the difference between a lie and an incomplete truth was mostly a question of the order in which information was presented. I intended to tell my team everything. I intended to do it after I had the new data in hand.

There were three of them. Halvorsen I've mentioned — he was the sedimentologist on the cruise, and he accepted the explanation with the mild professional interest of a man whose work was not directly affected by it. The other two were Ragnhild, a second-year PhD student doing her first offshore posting, who had the alert, slightly exhausted look of someone discovering that fieldwork is considerably more logistically complicated than labwork, and Magnus, a data technician who had been on the Lofoten for four years and who had developed, over those four years, the specific competence of a person who has seen researchers get excited about things that turned out to be nothing and had calibrated his own enthusiasm accordingly.

Magnus, in particular, I was not looking forward to telling.

* * *

The Bear Island run had gone smoothly. Fourteen days of baseline seismic work on the ridge system north of Bear Island, nothing anomalous, clean data filed and certified. Then we turned south, toward the Mohns Ridge, toward 73.17 North and 11.43 East, and I went back to the data deck and did not sleep very much.

We reached the survey coordinates on the morning of the fourth day. The sea was flat and grey, a light wind from the west, visibility to the horizon. I had the survey system configured and running before Halvorsen arrived.

"Same coordinates as last time?" he said, looking at the screen.

"Within about two kilometres," I said. "I want to do a grid pass. Four transects, centred on the anomaly location."

He looked at the grid I'd drawn. "That's a lot of coverage for a follow-up."

"I want to rule out localised geological source." This was true. It was also incomplete.

He nodded and went to his own station. I watched the depth display come up as the towed array deployed — the ridge topography resolving into the familiar false-colour map, the Mohns Ridge rising in greens and blues beneath us, and somewhere below all of it, 4,200 metres of dark water and whatever was at the bottom of it.

We began the first transect at 09.14.

* * *

I ran the spectral analysis on the live feed rather than the recorded data. This was an operational change from standard practice — normally the analysis ran in post-processing, after the survey, because running it live created a significant computational load on the data deck systems. I had made this change without announcing it. Magnus noticed immediately.

"Live spectral?" He looked at my screen, then at me, with the expression of a man who has seen this kind of thing before and is deciding how much to say about it.

"I want real-time monitoring of the low-frequency range," I said. "The anomaly was in background noise. I don't want to miss it if it appears briefly."

He looked at the screen for another moment. Then he went back to his station without comment. Magnus's silences had a texture to them. This one meant: I am going to watch what you do very carefully.

The first transect took forty minutes. Nothing.

The second transect passed two kilometres east of the original anomaly site. Nothing on the live spectral. I watched the frequency band I was looking for — the range where the original sequence had appeared — and it was clean. Background noise. The standard ambient profile of a Norwegian Sea deep-ridge environment in summer.

I rechecked my filter parameters. Everything was correct.

The third transect was the one that passed directly over 11.43 East. I knew it when the depth display showed the ridge dropping away beneath us toward the hadal floor. I had the spectral analysis display on full, the relevant frequency band highlighted. The ship ran on its standard heading at standard survey speed. The towed array dragged its sensors through the dark water two hundred metres below the hull.

At 14.07, the sequence appeared.

* * *

It was stronger than before. Not dramatically — this was not a signal that announced itself. But where the original detection had been faint enough that I'd had to run the analysis three times to be certain it was there, this one resolved clearly on the first pass. Six pulses, the long pause — and then, where the second group should have begun, nothing. And then, eleven seconds after the calibration ping fired at the end of the transect, one more pulse. Alone. In the silence where the second group should have been.

I stared at the display.

The ship moved on its heading. The survey continued. The towed array swept its sensors across the floor of the Norwegian Sea, and the spectral analysis programme ran its filters, and on the live display the frequency band showed background noise again. As though nothing had happened.

I ran a timestamp correlation against the survey log. The pulse had arrived eleven seconds after the Lofoten's hull-mounted sonar had completed its routine depth-calibration ping — fired automatically mid-transect, triggered by a position fix from the navigation system. It was a standard operational event. It happened on every survey. It happened at the same time every time.

I sat with this for a long time.

The calibration ping was in a completely different frequency range from the sequence. It was a standard multibeam pulse, the kind used by hundreds of research vessels in dozens of ocean basins every day of the year. There was no obvious acoustic relationship between the ping and the sequence's frequency range. They were not the same kind of signal.

But the sequence had shifted.

The interval between the calibration ping and the solitary pulse was eleven seconds. The time elapsed between the long pause beginning and that pulse was also eleven seconds.

Not six pulses and six pulses. Six pulses, a long pause, and then one — arriving where the second group should have been, eleven seconds after we made a sound.

I ran the fourth transect. We passed two kilometres west of the anomaly site. Nothing.

I requested that Magnus run a repeat of the third transect — standard survey procedure when you have a suspect result, common enough that it didn't require explanation. He ran it without comment.

On the repeat pass, the sequence appeared again. Same position, same strength. Six pulses, the long pause — and then silence where the second group should have been. This time, I watched the calibration ping fire and counted the seconds. At eleven seconds, the solitary pulse arrived.

Then silence.

I did not tell Magnus what I was looking at. I did not tell Halvorsen. I closed the live spectral display, flagged the data for detailed post-processing, and noted in the survey log that the follow-up survey had produced results consistent with the original anomaly detection and that further analysis was required. This was true. It was also the most dramatically understated sentence I have ever written in a survey log.

Ragnhild, who had been working quietly at the back of the data deck on her own dataset, looked up when I filed the note. She said: "Did you find what you were looking for?"

I said: "I found what was there." Which was not the same thing, and she was young enough that she accepted it as an answer.

* * *

That evening, after dinner, I went to the stern deck and called Yuna.

She picked up on the second ring, as she always did. Yuna Park operated on a relationship with her phone that I had always found slightly alarming — she answered immediately, regardless of time or circumstance, with a quality of attention that suggested she had simply been waiting for whoever was about to call. She was thirty-one years old, seven years younger than me, and she was a linguist, which meant she spent her professional life thinking about the ways that meaning was encoded and transmitted, which was either a very good or a very bad qualification for the conversation I was not quite about to have with her.

She said: "You've been on the water again."

"Bear Island baseline. We extended the return leg."

"Extended why?"

"Follow-up survey."

A pause. Yuna's pauses were not the same as other people's pauses. They were a specific kind of active silence, the way a good listener's silence is not neutral but attentive. "The thing you found," she said. "The thing you weren't going to tell me about yet."

"I found it again."

She didn't say anything.

"Stronger," I said. "And it — " I stopped. I was standing at the stern rail of the Lofoten, looking at the sea. The sky in the north was still light, a last diffuse brightness above the horizon. Below us, 3,100 metres. "It responded to something we did," I said. "Not directly. Not obviously. But the timing shifted when we made a sound. Eleven seconds after a calibration ping, it added a pulse that wasn't part of the original sequence."

A longer pause this time. Then Yuna said, carefully: "When you say responded."

"I mean the interval changed in correlation with our acoustic output. I'm not saying anything more than that yet."

"Mara."

"I know."

"What does the pattern look like? Structurally. If you had to describe its architecture."

This was very Yuna. Someone else would have asked what I thought it was, or whether I was certain, or whether I'd slept. Yuna asked what the structure looked like. It was why, of all the people I might have called, I had called her. "Regular intervals," I said. "Fixed duration. Six pulses, then a pause exactly double the interval — and then, where the second group should have begun, one pulse. Arriving eleven seconds after we made a sound."

"Double," she said. She said it the way she said things that interested her, which was quietly, without inflection, as though she were writing it down inside her own head.

"I haven't published the first detection. Langvik thinks it's instrument error."

"But you don't."

"No."

"And now it responded to a sound you made."

"The timing correlation is consistent across two passes. I'm going to run the full post-processing analysis tonight."

She was quiet for a moment. I listened to the sea and the hum of the Lofoten's engines.

She said: "I'm not going to ask you what you think it is. I can tell you already know and aren't saying, and I think that's probably right." Another pause. "But when you're ready to tell me, I want to understand the structure. The interval architecture. Whatever linguistic analogues there might be." A beat. "If that's the right word."

"I don't know if it's the right word yet."

"No," she said. "But I think you're starting to wonder."

I did not answer that. We talked for another twenty minutes about other things — her current research project, a conference she was presenting at in Stockholm, whether I had eaten anything that wasn't soup. When I hung up, the northern sky had finally, reluctantly, begun to darken.

I went back to the data deck. Magnus had left for the night. The screens were running on automatic, logging the survey's background data with the untroubled efficiency of a system that did not care what it was recording.

I sat down and started the post-processing analysis. I worked through until 03.30, when I had what I needed, and then I sat for a while longer looking at the results.

The sequence was there. Stronger than the first detection, cleaner, unmistakable. The interval structure was identical to the original. The additional pulse was real — it was in the waveform data, not an artifact, not a resonance, not instrument error — and it had arrived eleven seconds after the calibration ping. On both passes.

I wrote in my journal: The timing shift is consistent and reproducible. The sequence responded to external acoustic stimulus. I do not know what this means. I know what it cannot mean, which is any of the things I have been trained to assume.

I closed the journal. I made tea.

Outside, the Norwegian Sea ran north toward the pole, and somewhere below it, at a depth where the pressure was four hundred atmospheres and the temperature was just above freezing and the dark was total and absolute, something had heard us.

SIX

Convergence

The USS Thresher Point was a surveillance support vessel — not combat, not conspicuously naval, capable of being logged in Norwegian maritime records as a geophysical survey contractor without raising questions that anyone would pursue. She was 58 metres, low-slung, with a wide working deck aft and a sensor suite below the waterline that bore no relationship to anything a commercial survey contractor would operate. She had been in the Norwegian Sea for six days when Reyes came aboard at Tromsø, and she was already three days into the debris search when they reached the coordinates of Aurora Seven's last known position.

There was no debris.

This was not a surprise. The search and rescue operation had run for eleven days before being stood down, and the Norwegian Coast Guard had used assets that were considerably better than anything Reyes had available to him on the Thresher Point. If there was anything on the surface or near-surface to find, it had been found, or had drifted far enough in six weeks that finding it now would require a search area too large for their operational window. Reyes had not expected to find debris. What he had come for was the seafloor.

Lieutenant Eriksson — his navigation officer, Norwegian, seconded from the Royal Norwegian Navy to what her orders described as a joint maritime safety evaluation — had the side-scan sonar running from their first morning on site. The side-scan was the right tool for the initial pass: it covered more ground faster than the multibeam, and what Reyes wanted first was a picture of the seafloor in a two-kilometre radius around the loss position. He wanted to see if there was a hull down there, or hull fragments, or anything that looked like what a 14,000-tonne semi-submersible looked like after it reached the bottom of the Norwegian Sea.

The side-scan, after two and a half days, had found nothing that matched.

"Nothing consistent with structural debris," Eriksson said, on the morning of the third day. She had a precise, underdecorated way of speaking that Reyes found professionally useful. "The ridge topography is complex in the northwest quadrant — there's a canyon section that could conceal larger fragments — but the acoustic signature isn't consistent with steel on basalt."

"What does the acoustic signature say it is?"

"Sediment. Consolidated. Standard hadal floor composition for this section of the ridge." She paused. "Either the rig isn't there, or it's in a section of the seafloor we can't resolve with the side-scan."

Neither answer tells me much," Reyes said.

She looked at him briefly. "No," she agreed. "It doesn't."

* * *

He had spent the two days of the debris search reading documentation. The full set of files from NordDepth's server, the Norwegian Coast Guard's acoustic survey data, the records of the two earlier deep-survey operations in the area that had reported anomalous sonar returns. He had read all of it twice and parts of it three times, and the shape of what he was looking at had become, gradually, clearer — not the content, which remained unclear, but the shape.

The shape was this: a location in the Norwegian Sea, at a specific depth on a specific section of the Mohns Ridge, that had been producing low-frequency acoustic anomalies for at least eighteen months — longer, possibly, since the earlier surveys hadn't specifically been looking for them and might have classified similar signals without noting them. The signals had appeared in the records of three independent operations across that period, each time classified as background noise by automated systems operating below the threshold of human attention. Each time filed and forgotten.

Except Aurora Seven's environmental log, which had eleven entries over forty-three days, increasing in frequency until the rig went dark.

He had a theory. He was not yet willing to call it a theory. He was willing to call it a direction.

The direction was: the anomaly preceded the loss. The anomaly increased in frequency before the loss. The rig disappeared without a trace, without a distress signal, without a debris field. These three facts did not have a conventional explanation that connected them. Reyes was interested in unconventional explanations, but only once he'd thoroughly ruled out all the conventional ones, and he was not yet finished ruling them out.

He had one conventional explanation left to check. It required getting the Thresher Point's own acoustic sensors into the water above the loss position and running them in the frequency range the Aurora Seven's environmental log had documented.

He had saved this for last deliberately. Once he had that data, he would know whether the signal was still there. And knowing that would change something about how he was able to think about everything else.

* * *

He ran the acoustic survey on the morning of the third day, using the Thresher Point's towed hydrophone array — a passive system, designed for deep listening rather than active sonar. He set the frequency range to cover the band documented in the Aurora Seven logs, with a margin on either side. He deployed the array, reduced the ship's speed to minimum steerage, and waited.

For forty minutes, the array returned the ambient acoustic profile of the Norwegian Sea: the low continuous rumble of distant shipping, the faint biological scatter of the water column, the sub-audible groan of the ridge geology, the white noise of the current against the hydrophone casing. Nothing anomalous. The frequency band Reyes was watching showed only the standard background floor.

Then, at 10.15, the hydrophone array registered a signal.

It was brief. Eighty-three seconds, which Reyes recognised the moment he saw the duration logged — that number was already in his margin notes, written twice in the documentation from the Aurora Seven log. The signal was in the correct frequency range. Its intensity was below the array's alert threshold, which was why the automated system had not flagged it. Reyes was watching the live display, not waiting for flags.

He watched it appear and run its 83 seconds and stop. Then he looked at the playback waveform for a long time.

The waveform had interval structure. He could see it even in the compressed display — a pattern of pulses, regular, the gaps between them consistent. He couldn't resolve the detail at this scale. He would need the full post-processing analysis to characterise it properly.

But it was there.

The same signal that Aurora Seven's environmental monitoring system had logged and classified as background noise, eleven times over forty-three days, was present and active in the water below them right now.

Reyes closed the live display. He pulled up the post-processing queue and set the 10.15 detection to run at highest priority. Then he went to find Eriksson.

* * *

She was on the bridge, updating the navigation log. He said: "What's our current AIS traffic?"

AIS was the Automatic Identification System — the transponder-based tracking network that all commercial vessels above a certain tonnage were required to broadcast on, which meant that any ship in their vicinity with AIS active would appear on Eriksson's navigation display.

She pulled up the display without asking why. "One tanker, bearing two-seven-zero, approximately forty kilometres. Norwegian flagged, bound for Hammerfest." She scrolled. "And a research vessel, bearing one-four-five. Approximately two kilometres."

"Research vessel."

"Appears to be running a survey pattern. Slow transects, consistent heading changes. She's been in the area since at least this morning." Eriksson looked at the contact. "She's running a towed array. I can see the sonar return from the cable."

"What's her identification?"

Eriksson ran the AIS query. "RV Lofoten. Registered to the Birkeland Institute of Marine Sciences, Tromsø. Scientific research vessel, 73 metres." She glanced at him. "Norwegian."

Reyes looked at the bearing marker on the display. Two kilometres, bearing one-four-five. Running slow transects. Towed array deployed.

A Norwegian research vessel from a Tromsø marine sciences institute, running a deep-survey pattern two kilometres from the position where the Aurora Seven had disappeared, at the same time that his own acoustic array had just picked up the signal he'd come looking for.

He considered this for a moment.

"Log her," he said. "Standard maritime contact entry. Position, identification, course, speed."

"Already done," Eriksson said.

"Good." He looked at the bearing marker for another second. "Carry on."

He went back below to wait for the post-processing results.

* * *

The analysis came back at 19.40. He read it in his cabin, door closed, with a cup of coffee that went cold while he was reading.

The signal was not identical to what Aurora Seven's logs had recorded. The Aurora Seven system had captured only summary data — duration and intensity — because the raw waveform wasn't preserved for below-threshold detections. What Reyes had now was the actual waveform, and the waveform told him considerably more than the summaries had.

The signal had internal structure. Pulses, as he'd suspected from the compressed display. The interval between pulses was consistent to within a fraction of a second across the 83-second duration. The pulses themselves had a specific shape — not a simple spike, but a more complex form, with a rise time and a decay pattern that repeated with the same precision as the intervals.

He had a degree in electrical engineering before his commission, and had spent the first decade of his naval career in signals intelligence before moving into deep-sea acoustic operations. He looked at the waveform analysis and he thought about what kind of source produced signals with this character — with this internal regularity, this repetition precision, this interval consistency — and he ran through the list of natural sources he was aware of and eliminated them one by one.

Geological: no. Geological acoustic sources were continuous or episodic, driven by physical processes that were variable by nature. This signal's internal consistency was incompatible with geological origin.

Biological: no. He'd looked at the frequency range, the pulse shape, the interval structure. Nothing in the known acoustic biology of the Norwegian Sea produced signals with this character at this depth. The closest analogue — cetacean communication — operated at different frequencies, with different temporal structures, and was associated with surface or mid-water activity, not the hadal zone.

Anthropogenic: possible, but the signal's bearing had placed it directly below the vessel, at hadal depth, in a location with no mapped human infrastructure. No pipelines, no cables, no known installations.

He sat with what remained after he'd eliminated the conventional explanations. He didn't write it down. He wasn't ready to write it down.

He thought instead about the research vessel two kilometres to the southeast, running slow transects with a towed array. Birkeland Institute of Marine Sciences. He thought about the pattern of anomalous sonar returns in this area over the past eighteen months, returns that had been classified as background noise and never formally investigated.

He thought: someone from a marine sciences institute in Tromsø, running a survey in this specific location, at this specific time, is either here by coincidence or here for a reason.

He thought about coincidences. He didn't have a policy against them. He had found, in twenty-two years of practice, that genuine coincidences existed but were rarer than they appeared, and that the most reliable method for distinguishing them from non-coincidences was to look more carefully at the data.

He put the analysis report in his encrypted files. He finished the cold coffee. He pulled up the Norwegian research vessel registry and searched for the Lofoten's current registered scientific programme.

It took him eleven minutes to find the anomaly report filed by a Dr. M. Voss of the Birkeland Institute six weeks earlier. The coordinates in the report were 73.17 North, 11.43 East.

He read the report twice. Under Probable cause, it said: Unknown.

He put his laptop down and looked at the bulkhead for a moment.

Two kilometres to the southeast, on a research vessel he could see on the navigation display as a small green triangle moving slowly through its survey pattern, someone had filed an anomaly report at these exact coordinates, called the cause unknown, and come back for a second look.

He did not know yet what Dr. M. Voss had found. He did not know whether it was the same thing he had found. He did not know whether she had any idea that a US Navy support vessel was running its own acoustic survey two kilometres off her port quarter.

He knew that neither of them was here for the reason they had told anyone they were here.

He noted the name in his log. Then he went back to the acoustic analysis and kept reading.

SEVEN

Patterns

We returned to Tromsø on a Thursday. The Lofoten was back at her berth by noon, and by two o'clock I was in the institute's server room, copying the full survey dataset to my workstation. I told Halvorsen I was starting the post-processing and that I'd have the preliminary analysis report ready by end of week. He said fine. He had his own data to process and no particular reason to watch me work.

I did not start with the post-processing. I started with the archive.

I have a specific relationship with archives. This is, I think, an occupational condition rather than a personal one — the deep-survey work I do is inherently longitudinal, concerned with change over time, which means that any anomaly has to be understood not just as a thing that exists now but as a thing that may have existed before, that may have a history in the record if you go back far enough and look in the right places. Every anomaly I have ever investigated, I have started by asking: when did this begin?

The question here was slightly different. The question here was not when the sequence had begun — I had no way of knowing that, and pursuing it would require a systematic review of deep-survey data from across the Norwegian Sea going back decades, which was a project for another time. The question I needed to answer first was simpler and more specific.

The sequence had been interrupted by our calibration ping. The second group never arrived. Something had answered the ping instead. I had established that. What I had not established was whether this was a response to any acoustic pulse in the relevant frequency range, or a response to something specific about our calibration ping — its frequency signature, its intensity, its particular pattern. And to answer that, I needed to go back to the moment it had first appeared.

The first detection had been on the survey run two months ago, in the background noise of the Lofoten's deep-ridge data. I had recorded it during a transect that passed directly over the anomaly site. Which meant — if the response mechanism I'd observed was consistent — that a mid-transect calibration ping had fired, and eleven seconds later the second group had been replaced by a solitary pulse.

I pulled up the original survey log. I found the transect. I found the calibration ping timestamp.

Then I went back further. If the sequence responded to our calibration ping on this cruise, had it responded to calibration pings on previous cruises? And if so — I felt something tighten in my chest as I framed the question — had we been triggering responses for longer than three months without knowing it?

* * *

The Lofoten's survey archive goes back eleven years, to the vessel's commissioning. Every survey run is logged, every instrument event timestamped, every sonar pulse recorded. I had access to all of it. I had read significant portions of it over the years, looking for things I'd missed. I had never looked at it with this specific question in mind.

I filtered the archive to show only surveys that had passed within five kilometres of 73.17 North, 11.43 East. There were fourteen of them, going back to the Lofoten's second operating year. I pulled the environmental monitoring logs for each one — the background noise recordings that ran continuously during all survey operations — and set my spectral analysis programme to scan them for signals in the anomaly's frequency range.

The search ran for two hours. I made coffee and sat at my desk and did not think about what I might find, because thinking about what you might find before you find it is a form of contamination. You look at the result you hoped for and you see it in data that doesn't support it. I had made this mistake once, early in my career, and I had learned from it with sufficient thoroughness that I hadn't made it since.

When the search completed, I looked at the results for a long time before I let myself understand them.

The anomaly was in six of the fourteen surveys. Not the same six every time — there was a gap in the middle years, three consecutive surveys with nothing, and then it reappeared. The earliest detection was four years ago. The most recent, before my own original find, was eighteen months ago, in a routine baseline survey that Halvorsen had led in my absence. That survey's environmental log showed two detections, both classified as background noise by the automated system, neither reviewed by a human. The file had been certified and archived with a green checkmark.

I stared at that entry for a moment. Halvorsen had been standing two kilometres above this thing and hadn't known it was there. His system had logged it twice and he'd never seen either entry. Why would he? Nobody reviewed background noise logs unless they were specifically looking for something, and nobody had been specifically looking for something here because nobody had known to look.

I wrote the earliest detection date in my notebook. Four years ago. Then I wrote the most recent. Then I wrote the count: six of the fourteen passes had produced detections, all within the past four years. The frequency had been increasing over that period. Early on: one detection in four passes. More recently: four detections in four passes.

Whatever was down there had been present and producing signals for at least four years. It had been producing them more consistently as time passed.

I closed the notebook. I made more coffee. I stood at the window of the analysis room and looked at the harbour for a long time.

* * *

The 2019 survey.

This was the piece I had not yet looked at, and I had not yet looked at it because I already suspected what I would find, and I wanted to be certain before I allowed myself to believe it.

In 2019, the Lofoten had run a deep-ridge survey along the Mohns Ridge that included a pass directly over the anomaly site. I had been on that cruise. I had been the lead geophysicist. I had reviewed the data, found nothing anomalous in my initial pass, signed off on the survey, and filed the results. The results were in the archive. They had been certified with a green checkmark. They were, to all official record, clean.

That survey was also the one during which the Lofoten had performed a routine instrument calibration in the middle of the transit — a standard multibeam sonar calibration, conducted at a specific frequency, at a specific position along the survey track.

I pulled up the calibration log. The calibration had been conducted at 14.23 on August 7th, 2019. The position at the time of calibration: 73.16 North, 11.44 East. Half a kilometre from the anomaly site.

I pulled up the 2019 environmental monitoring log for the same timestamp.

There were two entries.

The first: logged earlier in the transect, before the calibration. Low-frequency acoustic detection. Duration: 37 seconds. Source unknown. Intensity: below alert threshold. Classification: background noise.

The second: at 14.23.11 — eleven seconds after the calibration pulse. Low-frequency acoustic detection. Duration: 3 seconds. Source unknown. Intensity: below alert threshold. Classification: background noise.

I sat down.

Two entries. Two detections. The earliest signals the Lofoten's systems had ever recorded from this location.

The first I had missed entirely. The second had come eleven seconds after we'd sent a calibration pulse.

I had been the lead geophysicist. I had reviewed this data. I had signed off on it and filed it and put a green checkmark on it and gone home.

It had been there the whole time.

* * *

I want to describe what I felt when I understood this, and I find that I cannot do it with full accuracy because full accuracy would require a precision I don't have about my own internal states. What I can say is that it was not what people in books feel when they make discoveries.

There was no exhilaration. There was no sense of the world opening. There was something closer to the feeling of stepping through a door you have been approaching for a long time and finding yourself in a room that is much larger than you expected, and much darker, and realising that you cannot see the walls.

We had sent the signal. In 2019, during a routine instrument calibration on a routine survey cruise that I had personally led, the Lofoten had emitted a sonar pulse at a specific frequency. And something at 4,200 metres depth, at 73.17 North, 11.43 East, had received that pulse and eleven seconds later had replied.

And we had logged the reply as background noise. I had signed off on the survey. The file had been filed. The green checkmark had been applied.

For four years after that, the sequence had appeared intermittently in the data of every survey that passed nearby — sometimes strong, sometimes faint, but present. Paired entries, every time: a longer detection earlier in the transect, a brief solitary pulse eleven seconds after a calibration ping. The same pattern. Logged. Filed. Certified clean.

For four years, the Lofoten's automated systems had been classifying it as background noise. And for four years, nobody — including me, the person who had been specifically looking for anomalies in this data — had made the connection.

I thought about this for a long time. Then I thought about what it meant.

* * *

It meant we had not discovered something. We had caused something. The 2019 calibration pulse had not been the first signal the anomaly had ever received from a human source — there were too many research vessels and commercial ships that transited this area for that to be plausible. But it had been the signal that triggered the first documented response. Which meant the response mechanism was not to all acoustic stimuli. It was selective It was responding to something specific about the calibration sequence — its frequency structure, its interval pattern, or some combination of the two that I hadn't yet fully characterised.

And it had been responding, intermittently and consistently, for four years. Without anyone noticing.

I thought about who I could tell.

This was not a rhetorical exercise. I went through the list of people with any plausible claim on this information and assessed each one in turn.

Langvik: I had already told Langvik, in the most carefully prepared presentation I was capable of, that there was something anomalous here, and he had said instrument error. Telling Langvik again, with more data, would produce one of two outcomes: he would say instrument error again, more firmly, with the specifically unyielding quality that institutional dismissal acquires when it has already been delivered once, or he would take it seriously, which meant it would immediately become the institute's finding rather than mine and would be managed in ways I could not control and did not trust. Either outcome was worse than my current position.

Halvorsen: a careful man, a decent scientist, and someone who had been running surveys over this location for years without seeing what was in his own data. I did not think this reflected badly on him — the anomaly was not visible without specifically looking for it in the way I had been looking. But telling him would require explaining why I had not told him before, which would require explaining what I had and had not told him on the survey cruise, which would be a complicated and probably professionally damaging conversation.

The Norwegian Maritime Authority, or any other regulatory or governmental body: I had nothing yet that constituted publishable evidence. I had archival correlations and a timing pattern and a strong inference. In the current state of the analysis, any official body I approached would classify this as speculative and either file it or investigate it in ways I could not control.

I went through the rest of the list. I concluded, methodically and without particular drama, that the answer was nobody. Not yet. What I needed first was more data, and what I needed the data to tell me was the one thing I had been carefully not saying, to myself or anyone else, since three o'clock in the morning on a research vessel two months ago.

I needed to understand what, specifically, the 2019 calibration pulse was. Not just its frequency and intensity — those I had. I needed to understand whether there was something else about it: something in its structure, its duration, its modulation pattern, that might explain why it had produced a response when so many other acoustic events in this location had apparently not.

I spent two more hours running that analysis.

* * *

At 23.14, I found it.

The 2019 calibration pulse had been a standard multibeam calibration, which meant it had used the Lofoten's standard calibration sequence: a series of frequency sweeps at fixed intervals, run in a specific order. The sequence was the same on every Lofoten calibration, because it was generated by the calibration software and the software ran the same routine every time. I had run this calibration myself, on that cruise, without giving it any thought, because it was as automatic as checking the engine oil.

But the 2019 calibration had a specific property that I had not noticed until now, and that the calibration software itself would have had no reason to flag: the interval structure of the frequency sweeps — the gap between each sweep in the sequence — was, when expressed in seconds, 4.3 seconds between each sweep and 8.6 seconds at the sequence boundary. A ratio of two to one.

The same ratio. The same intervals. Not a structural parallel — an exact match.

The anomaly's pulse architecture used 4.3 seconds between pulses and 8.6 seconds for the long pause between groups. The calibration sequence used 4.3 seconds between sweeps and 8.6 seconds at its boundary. We had sent it its own language. Not approximately. Exactly.

I looked at this for a very long time.

The calibration sequence had a two-to-one interval structure. The anomaly's pulse architecture had a two-to-one interval structure. The anomaly had first appeared eleven seconds after the calibration pulse — not as a random response to acoustic noise, but as a reply to something it had recognised. In the four years since, the paired pattern had appeared consistently: a sequence beginning unprompted, interrupted at the long pause, answered eleven seconds after each calibration ping.

The calibration hadn't just triggered a response. The calibration pulse had been, in some sense I did not yet understand, a signal the anomaly recognised. And it had replied in kind — using the same structural ratio, the same interval architecture, the same mathematical relationship encoded in the thing we had accidentally sent.

We had sent a signal. It had answered. And for four years we had been having a conversation we didn't know we were having, in a language we hadn't known we spoke.

* * *

I sat in the analysis room for a long time. The building was empty. Through the window the harbour was dark, the Lofoten at her berth, the water very still.

I did not panic. I want to be precise about this because I think it is important and because I think it would be easy to mistake what I felt for composure, which it was not. It was something more specific than composure: a kind of enforced methodical attention, the same mode I used when I was working through a difficult dataset and needed to stay focused on the next step rather than the implications of the step after that.

I thought about the next step.

The next step was not publishing, which I could not do yet. The next step was not telling Langvik, for the reasons I'd already enumerated. The next step was not contacting any official body, for the same reasons.

The next step was telling Yuna.

Not because Yuna was a geophysicist — she wasn't; she was a linguist, and what I had found was not, in any conventional sense, a linguistics problem. But because the thing I was looking at — a signal with internal structure, with interval ratios, with a consistent response to acoustic stimulus — was not only a geophysics problem either. It was a problem about communication. About encoding. About what it might mean for something to reply to a pulse using the same structural language as the original pulse.

Yuna had said, on the phone from the Lofoten's stern deck: I want to understand the structure. The interval architecture. Whatever linguistic analogues there might be, if that's the right word.

I thought: it might be the right word.

I thought: I need her to look at this.

I thought: I am going to need to tell her everything.

It was past midnight. I turned off the analysis room lights, locked my workstation, and walked out of the institute into the quiet Tromsø night. The sky was beginning to darken now, a month past midsummer, the first real dark of the summer asserting itself in the northern sky.

I walked home. I did not call Yuna that night — it was too late, and I needed to think about how to say what I was going to say, because what I was going to say was something I had not said to anyone, and I needed to say it right.

I sat at my kitchen table for a long time. Then I went to my desk and started writing down everything, from the beginning, in order.

It took most of the night. When I had finished, I read it back. It was all there: the detection, the archive search, the 2019 calibration, the ratio. All of it, in order, stated as precisely as I was able.

I read the last page twice. Then I put the notebook in the drawer, locked it, and went to make coffee.

Whatever was at 4,200 metres below the Norwegian Sea had been waiting, in some form, for four years. It had answered us once. It had answered us again. Whatever came next was going to require a kind of thinking I could not do alone.

I called Yuna at seven in the morning. She picked up on the second ring.

EIGHT

First Contact (Between Humans)

He called the institute first. This I found out later, after the fact, in the way you find out the things that happened before you knew a story was beginning — reconstructed, assembled from what he told me and what I could infer, until I had a sequence that was probably accurate.

He had called the Birkeland Institute switchboard and asked to be connected to the office of Dr. M. Voss. The switchboard had told him that Dr. Voss was not in the building that day. He had asked whether she could be reached and the switchboard had told him, with the specific brand of bureaucratic neutrality that Scandinavian institutional offices have developed to a high art, that they were not able to give out staff contact details to members of the public. He had left his name and a number and asked that the message be passed on.

I received the message two days later, on a Wednesday morning. The slip of paper said: Eli Reyes. A US phone number. Message: Would appreciate a conversation about research in the Norwegian Sea. I read it twice, put it in my pocket, and went to give a seminar on deep-ridge seismic methodology to a group of master's students who had not asked to be there and whose attention was divided among my slides, their phones, and the window.

After the seminar I went to my office and looked at the phone number for a while.

Reyes was a common enough surname. The message was anodyne. Research in the Norwegian Sea covered a substantial portion of everything I had done for twelve years. There was nothing in the slip of paper that was, on its face, alarming.

I thought about the research vessel I had noticed on our navigation display during the follow-up survey — unregistered, running what Halvorsen had logged as a parallel survey track. Two kilometres from our position. I had not thought about it much at the time. I was thinking about it now.

I did not call the number that day. I ran the name through the public naval registry, which returned a Commander Eli Reyes, US Navy, deep-sea operations, based at Naval Station Norfolk. I sat with that for an evening. Then I called back.

* * *

He answered on the first ring, which meant he had been waiting.

"Dr. Voss," he said. "Thank you for calling."

"Commander Reyes." I had decided in advance to use the rank. It was a form of information: I know who you are. It was also, I recognised, a form of nerves, which was less useful but harder to suppress.

A brief pause. Then: "You did your homework."

"You left your name."

"Fair enough." His voice was even, slightly dry, with the quality of someone who chose his words by elimination rather than addition. "I'm going to be in Oslo next week. I'd like to meet in person, if you're willing. Nothing formal. I'll buy the coffee."

I said: "What's this about?"

He said: "I think you know what it's about. And I think you'd prefer to discuss it somewhere that isn't a phone line."

He was right on both counts. I said I'd meet him. He named a café near the university, a time, a day. We hung up.

I sat in my office for a long time after that. On my screen, the spectral analysis of the second survey's waveform data was open, the familiar pattern of pulses resolved in false colour, the seventh pulse's timing correlation annotated in red. I had looked at this data so many times in the past weeks that I could reconstruct it from memory. I knew every feature of it the way you know a piece of music you've played until it's in your hands.

I closed the display. I thought about what I was going to say to a US Navy officer who had been running an acoustic survey two kilometres from mine and who thought I knew what he wanted to talk about.

I thought: I know approximately half of what he wants to talk about. The question is whether he knows the other half.

* * *

The café was a small place, wooden tables, the particular smell of Oslo coffee that I associate with indoor November regardless of the season. I arrived six minutes early and chose a table at the back, facing the door. This was not, I told myself, tactical. It was a preference.

Reyes arrived at exactly the agreed time. I recognised him immediately — not from any photograph, because I hadn't found one; from the way he moved through the café, which was with the low-energy economy of someone accustomed to confined spaces and to being watched while pretending not to be. He was lean, dark-haired, in his mid-forties, wearing a grey jacket that was doing an unremarkable job of not looking like a uniform. He scanned the room, found me, and came directly to the table without stopping at the counter.

"Dr. Voss."

"Commander."

He sat down across from me. Up close he had the stillness I'd noticed from the description I'd built — the economy extended to his face, which was attentive without being expressive. He looked at me for a moment in a way that was not unfriendly but was very much an assessment.

"Coffee," he said. It wasn't a question. He raised a hand toward the counter.

"Please," I said.

He ordered, in serviceable Norwegian, two coffees. We waited. The café was half-full, the ambient noise sufficient. He had chosen well, I thought, and then recognised that I was thinking like someone in a negotiation, and that this was probably the correct register for what was about to happen.

The coffees arrived. He wrapped both hands around his cup and looked at me.

He said: "I'm going to tell you something true, and then I'm going to ask you a question, and I'd like you to consider answering it honestly even though you have no particular reason to trust me."

I said: "All right."

"I was on a vessel two kilometres from the Lofoten during your follow-up survey last month. Running acoustic monitoring at the same coordinates you were surveying."

I had known this, or suspected it, but hearing it stated was different from suspecting it. I kept my face still. "Go on," I said.

"My instruments detected a low-frequency signal at those coordinates. Consistent with signals logged in the environmental monitoring data of the Aurora Seven in the forty-three days before the rig disappeared." He paused. "The question: have you found the same signal?"

I looked at him. He looked back. We were, I realised, doing exactly the same thing — looking for the signs of someone who already knew the answer to the question they were asking.

I said: "Why should I tell you what I've found?"

"Because if what I found is what I think it is," he said, "then what you found is considerably larger than either of us can handle alone. And because you filed an anomaly report six weeks ago with the word 'Unknown' under probable cause, which means you already know that whatever it is, it doesn't fit any of the explanations you were trained to apply."

I said: "That's a reasonable inference from a public filing."

"It is," he said. "You could have put 'geological source' and nobody would have questioned it. You put 'Unknown.'"

I had not thought about the anomaly report that way — as a signal in itself, as a thing I'd sent out into the world that could be read by someone who was looking for exactly this kind of signal. The irony of this was not lost on me, though I did not say so.

I picked up my coffee. I said: "Tell me what you found."

* * *

He told me. He was precise about it — dates, frequencies, durations, the eleven entries in the Aurora Seven environmental log, the waveform analysis, the interval structure, the elimination of conventional sources. He did not editorialize. He did not reach for interpretations. He laid out the data in order and stopped when he reached the end of the data.

When he finished I said: "The interval structure of the pulses in the waveform. The gap between pulses and the long pause between groups — what was the relationship?"

He looked at me. Something shifted in his expression — not quite surprise, but a recalibration. "Two to one," he said. "Exactly."

I nodded slowly.

"That means something to you," he said.

"It means something to the data," I said. "Yes."

A pause. He was very still. "I've told you what I found," he said. "That was the deal."

"You haven't told me who sent you to those coordinates."

"No," he said. "I haven't."

"Then we're not fully trading yet."

He looked at me for a moment. Then, unexpectedly, something that might have been amusement appeared briefly at the corner of his mouth and was gone. "Fair point," he said. "I was assigned to investigate the disappearance of the Aurora Seven. The coordinates put me at the last known operational location of the rig. I am conducting what is officially a maritime safety audit."

"And unofficially?"

"Unofficially, I'm trying to understand why twenty-four people and a fourteen-thousand-tonne structure disappeared without leaving any evidence of what happened to them. And why the rig's environmental monitoring system logged the same signal eleven times in the forty-three days before it disappeared."

I thought about twenty-four people. I thought about what I knew and had been sitting with for weeks, alone, in an analysis room in Tromsø. I thought about all the reasons not to trust a US Navy officer I had met forty minutes ago.

Then I thought about the 2019 calibration pulse, and the four-year response history, and the two-to-one ratio, and the seventh pulse arriving eleven seconds after we made a sound.

I opened my laptop.

* * *

I showed him everything. Not summaries — the actual data, the waveform analysis, the archive search, the 2019 survey log with the calibration timestamp and the eleven-second gap to the first documented response. I showed him the spectral analysis, the interval structure, the response correlation across two survey passes. I showed him the two-to-one interval architecture — the 4.3 and 8.6 seconds encoded in both the anomaly's pulse structure and the 2019 calibration sequence — and what it meant that they matched exactly.

He looked at all of it without speaking. He had a way of reading data — leaning slightly forward, his coffee forgotten, his eyes moving across the display in a pattern that wasn't random — that I recognised because it was my own pattern. Attention distributed across the whole before focusing on the detail. Looking for the shape first.

When he reached the end he sat back. He was quiet for a moment.

"The 2019 calibration pulse was the trigger," he said. It was not a question.

"The first documented response was eleven seconds after the calibration. Every subsequent response has been consistent with calibration-type acoustic stimulus — pulses carrying the two-to-one interval structure."

"And you didn't notice it at the time."

"No. The response was below the automated alert threshold. It was logged as background noise and the survey was cleared." I paused. "I signed off on that survey."

He looked at me. There was nothing in his expression that suggested judgement. He said: "The Aurora Seven's environmental system logged eleven detections over forty-three days and classified all of them as background noise. Their operators signed off on it too."

"That's not the same thing."

"No," he said. "It isn't. But it's the same mechanism. Systems designed to filter signal from noise, doing exactly what they were designed to do, in a situation nobody designed them for."

He pulled out his own laptop. He showed me the Aurora Seven's environmental log — the full forty-three-day record, not just the six entries I'd read about in the publicly filed incident reports. I had not known about the earlier detections, the ones spread across the weeks before the rig disappeared. I had not known the frequency had been increasing.

I looked at the timeline he'd drawn in his notes. Forty-three days before. Then thirty-one. Twenty-two. Fourteen. Nine. Then the final six, compressed into fifty-eight hours.

"They were getting closer together," I said.

"Yes."

"The rig was logging the sequence more and more frequently in the weeks before it disappeared."

"Yes."

I looked at the data on both our screens. Mine and his. The same signal, documented from two angles, in two different datasets, by two people who hadn't known about each other until three weeks ago.

"Show me the waveform from your acoustic survey," I said.

He called it up. I compared it against my own. The interval structure was identical — the same ratio, the same pulse shape, the same duration. Not similar. Identical, within measurement tolerance.

The café around us was doing what cafés do: the espresso machine, the murmur of other conversations, a door opening and closing on the street outside. Normal things. The world going about its morning in the specific ordinary way that mornings go.

Reyes was looking at the two waveforms side by side on our screens.

"The same signal," he said, though neither of us needed to say it.

"Yes."

He was quiet for a long moment. I waited. Outside, Oslo went about its business, indifferent to us and to the data on our screens and to whatever was producing that data four thousand, two hundred metres below the surface of the Norwegian Sea.

Then Reyes said: "We need to go down there."

I looked at him.

He was looking back at me with the particular quality of attention of a person who has reached a conclusion and is waiting to find out if the other person has reached the same one.

I had reached the same one. I had been sitting with it for weeks, alone, in an analysis room, and I had been circling it the way you circle something that you know you're going to have to say out loud eventually and that will be different once you've said it. It would be different now. It was already different — he had said it, which meant it was in the room, which meant it was real in a way it hadn't quite been before.

I said: "Yes."

He nodded, once, as though we had agreed on something practical.

Which, I supposed, we had.

The coffee had gone cold. Neither of us had finished it. Outside the café windows, the Oslo morning was bright and ordinary, and somewhere north of us, below the Norwegian Sea, something had been answering our signals for four years.

We had a great deal to talk about.

ACT TWO

The Descent

NINE

Preparation

There is a specific kind of preparation that is about what you tell people and what you don't, and it is different from and considerably more exhausting than the ordinary kind. The ordinary kind — the logistics, the equipment checks, the scheduling — I could do in my sleep. I had been preparing survey operations for twelve years. I knew how to organise a vessel, how to brief a crew, how to file the requisite documentation with the institute and the Norwegian Maritime Authority and whoever else required notification of research activity in the Norwegian Sea.

The other kind required more thought.

The operation, as Reyes had constructed it through his institutional channels, was officially a wreck-site survey conducted under the auspices of the international maritime safety audit — his cover, still intact, still plausible. The DSV would go down to the last known position of the Aurora Seven, document whatever the seafloor survey had found or failed to find, and return. This was reasonable. This was defensible. This was the kind of operation that explained the presence of a US Navy-affiliated deep-submersible crew in Norwegian waters without requiring anyone to ask uncomfortable questions.

What the operation actually was, Reyes and I had agreed not to write down in any document that would appear in an operational brief.

The people who would be on the support vessel needed to know enough to do their jobs. They did not need to know more than that. This was not deception, I told myself. It was operational economy. It was the same principle Mara-of-three-months-ago had applied to her survey team on the Lofoten: tell them what's true, tell them what's relevant, don't tell them the part that will make the work impossible before it starts.

I was aware, preparing the brief, that this argument was becoming a habit.

* * *

The support vessel was the Lofoten. Reyes had made this request and I had not argued with it — she was the vessel I knew, she had the equipment we needed, and her presence in the area was explainable given my previous survey work. Langvik had approved the deployment against my remaining research allocation and a separate budget line Reyes had arranged through channels he described only as institutional. I had not asked for a more specific description. There were things about Reyes's institutional arrangements that I was making a practice of not examining closely, on the grounds that examining them closely would require me to have opinions about them, and having opinions about them would complicate the operation.

The crew was minimal: the Lofoten's standard complement of twelve, with Halvorsen standing down on a pre-arranged leave that I had organised without explaining why, and Magnus retained because he was too competent to replace and would make less trouble asking questions he hadn't been asked to ask than a stranger would. Ragnhild was gone — her posting had ended, and I was privately relieved not to have to manage a student's curiosity on top of everything else.

The DSV — a Triton 3300/3, rated to 3,300 metres with a three-person crew configuration — was operated by a Norwegian deep-sea services company that Reyes had contracted. One pilot: a Norwegian named Stig who had fourteen years of deep submersible experience and the specific unhurried confidence of people who routinely descended into places that would kill them if anything went wrong. Reyes and I would be the scientific observers, occupying the second and third seats.

The plan was one dive. Down to Aurora Seven's last known position, survey the seafloor in a two-kilometre radius, document what was there. Come up. Report what we'd found — the official version — to

Reyes's contacts at the maritime safety audit. Then decide, the two of us, what to do about the rest of it.

The rest of it was not in any document.

* * *

Yuna arrived in Tromsø on the Tuesday before departure, by train from Oslo, with a backpack and a canvas shoulder bag that contained, I knew without asking, at least three notebooks and a laptop and the specific assortment of books that she carried everywhere and that were never entirely the same books twice. She was thirty-one years old and slight and had the quality, rare in researchers of any kind, of giving the impression that she was always paying full attention to two things simultaneously — the conversation she was having and something just behind it, some pattern or structure that the conversation was generating and that she was quietly documenting.

She had agreed to come without asking many questions, which was characteristic. What she had asked, on the phone, was: am I going to need waders? And: is this a conference or fieldwork? I had said fieldwork, and she had said good, I prefer fieldwork, and that had been the extent of the negotiation.

I met her at the station. She looked at me for a moment when she came through the gate — one of those Yuna assessments, quick and complete — and said: "You look terrible."

"I haven't been sleeping well."

"Since when?"

"Since approximately June."

She fell into step beside me. "That's when you found it."

"Yes."

She didn't say anything else until we were in the car, and then she said: "Tell me everything. In order. Don't skip the technical parts."

This was also characteristic. Most people, when you tell them you've found something extraordinary in deep-sea survey data, want the summary. Yuna wanted the structure. She wanted to understand how you had arrived at the conclusion before she would allow herself to form one of her own.

I told her everything. It took forty minutes, which was the duration of the drive to the institute and the walk to the analysis room where I had the data loaded on the primary workstation. When I finished, she sat down in front of the screen and said nothing for several minutes. I let her look.

* * *

The first thing she said was: "The two-to-one ratio. Show me the original calibration sequence — not just the anomaly's response, the actual interval structure of the 2019 calibration sweep — the gap between sweeps and the boundary pause."

I showed her.

She looked at it for a long time. She said: "The calibration pulse has the ratio in its interval structure. The anomaly's own sequence has the same ratio in its architecture." She looked at me. "The response itself is just one pulse. But the thing that answered already spoke the same language as the thing that called."

"That's the inference."

"Not an inference," she said, quietly, still looking at the screen. "Or not only. The anomaly was already using this ratio in its own architecture — independently, before any contact. The calibration ping arrived carrying the same structure. And something answered. Not to other acoustic stimuli. To this one." She paused, and I could see her choosing the word with some care. "That's not a trigger and response. That's recognition. And recognition implies" — another pause — "a mind that was already listening for something it knew how to hear."

She was quiet for a moment. Then:

"Recognition — that's the technical term, in linguistic anthropology. When a communication system receives a novel signal and encodes an element of that signal's structure into its reply, that's not accidental resonance. It's not echo. It means the receiving system analysed the incoming signal's architecture before generating a response." She turned to look at me. "Mara. Whatever produced this didn't just hear the calibration pulse. It parsed it."

I had not said this to myself, not in those words, though I had been circling it for weeks. Hearing her say it — with the specific precision of someone who spent her professional life thinking about how communication systems worked — was different from circling it alone.

I said: "I know."

She said: "You know what this looks like."

"Yes."

"You've known for a while."

"Since the archive search. Since I found the 2019 entry."

She looked at me with an expression I couldn't immediately read. Not alarm — Yuna's face under genuine surprise was more interior than that, more focused. She said: "And you've been sitting with this alone."

"Until now."

"Until now," she repeated. She turned back to the screen. For a long moment she was simply quiet, looking at the waveforms — the 2019 calibration pulse and the anomaly's sequence, side by side, the structural similarity visible even without the spectral overlay. Then she said: "I'm going to need to run some analyses of my own. On the sequence's interval architecture across all documented detections — I want to map whether the structure has been shifting over time. Whether the ratio has held exactly or drifted. Whether anything new has appeared in the four years of archive data."

"You think it changed."

"I think everything changes." A pause. "I also think something that can recognise a signal's architecture is not simply waiting passively. If it's been transmitting for four years, I want to know whether those transmissions have been identical or whether they've been — " she paused — "developing." She looked at me again. "You should have called me in June."

"I wasn't ready."

"I know. I'm not scolding you." She smiled briefly, the particular Yuna smile that wasn't quite warm but was very much present. "I'm just noting that you could have called me in June."

* * *

Fifteen hundred kilometres south, in an office building in Bergen that faced the harbour, Aldric Moen received a call at eleven in the morning from a contact at the Norwegian Offshore Directorate whose value to him lay entirely in an ability to know which government agencies were doing what before the relevant press release had been drafted.

The contact told him that a joint maritime safety operation, operating under US Navy auspices with Norwegian cooperation, had deployed a deep-submersible vehicle to the last known position of the Aurora Seven. The deployment was logged as a wreck-site documentation survey. The DSV had gone into the water the previous morning.

Moen thanked the contact, ended the call, and stood at his window for a while looking at the harbour. A cargo vessel was moving slowly out of the eastern berth, low in the water, heavy with something he couldn't see.

He thought about the American naval officer who had come to his office six weeks ago and spent three hours in his documentation server and left saying only that he had found useful material. He thought about the frequency consistency his own engineering team had identified — the match between the anomalous sonar returns from previous surveys and the signals in Aurora Seven's environmental log. He thought about the eleven entries, the increasing frequency, the silence after the forty-third day.

He thought about twenty-four people.

He picked up his phone and made three calls: to his chief engineer, to his head of legal, and to the president of his board of directors. The calls were brief. What he said in each of them was different but what he meant was the same: something is happening at the Aurora Seven site. I don't know what it is yet. I need us to be ready for what it might be.

He did not say: I think this was not an accident.

He had been not saying this for six weeks. He was not certain how much longer he could continue not saying it.

* * *

The evening before departure, Reyes and I walked the Lofoten's deck together. It was a habit we'd developed in the two weeks of preparation — a nightly circuit, ostensibly checking that the survey equipment was properly stowed, actually a time when we talked without being overheard.

The sky was darkening, finally, genuinely, the way it only does in late August even this far north. The water was calm, the harbour lights beginning to assert themselves against the dusk.

Reyes said: "Your colleague. Yuna. She's good."

"Yes."

"The analysis she ran this afternoon — the temporal mapping across all detections. Did you see the drift?"

I had. Yuna had spent the afternoon running the interval structure of every documented detection through a comparative analysis. What she'd found was subtle but consistent: across the four years of documented signals, the interval between pulses had shortened by a small but measurable fraction. Not dramatically. Not in a way that altered the two-to-one ratio — that had held across all detections. But the rhythm had quickened, fractionally, over time.

"It's been changing," I said.

"Something that changes over four years is not geological," Reyes said.

"No."

We walked. The Lofoten shifted slightly at her moorings, the gentle hull-groan of a vessel not quite still.

Reyes said: "Tomorrow we'll know more."

"Yes."

"Are you ready?"

I thought about this. It was the kind of question that didn't have an honest yes as an answer, because what ready would mean in this context — ready to descend three kilometres into water that was answering our signals, ready to look with my own eyes at whatever was at the bottom of the Norwegian Sea, ready for the part where the data became something I could not unsee — was not a state I had achieved and was not certain I was capable of achieving.

"I don't think it matters," I said. "We need to go."

He looked at me briefly, something in his expression that was close to recognition. "No," he said. "It doesn't matter."

We finished the circuit. Below us the harbour was quiet and above us the sky was finally, uncommittedly dark, the stars beginning to appear one at a time in the order they always appear, the oldest light first.

I went to my cabin. I read for a while without taking anything in. I set my alarm and turned off the light.

I did not sleep for a very long time.

TEN

The Water

The DSV entered the water at 07.14 on a Thursday morning, lifted from the Lofoten's aft deck by crane and lowered until the hull touched the surface and the surface accepted it and we sank below the chop. I was in the observer seat, my back against the curved interior of the pressure sphere, my knees closer to the pilot's seat than was entirely comfortable. Stig was at the controls. Reyes was in the second observer position six inches to my left, close enough that I could feel the slight warmth of him in the cold of the sphere.

The DSV was a Triton 3300/3, which I had known from its specifications but which I now understood from the inside: a pressure sphere of borosilicate glass and titanium, 1.8 metres in diameter, attached to an open aluminium frame that held the thrusters and battery packs and equipment housings and the four powerful external lights that were, at this moment, showing me the surface of the Norwegian Sea from below.

It looked like hammered metal. That was my first thought — that the underside of the surface, seen from ten metres below it, looked like hammered pewter, or like the underside of a plate someone had struck repeatedly with a small tool, the light fragmenting and reforming in shifting patterns that had nothing to do with any surface I had seen before. It was beautiful in the way that fundamentally disorienting things are sometimes beautiful: the beauty was in the strangeness, and the strangeness was in the fact that this was a perspective the human eye was not designed to have.

I had been in submersibles before. Five times, in fifteen years of deep-sea work. I had never entirely acclimatised to this moment —

the moment after entry when the world above resolved into something alien and you understood, in your body rather than your mind, that you were now in a medium that was not yours.

Stig said, in Norwegian, that we were at ten metres and beginning our descent. I noted the time: 07.16.

* * *

The ocean has zones the way a building has floors, but the comparison fails immediately because the zones are not static and the boundaries between them are not fixed and the building has no equivalent of the specific quality of pressure that changes everything as you go deeper — not the dramatic crushing pressure of television deep-sea documentaries, which you don't feel because the sphere equalises, but the more abstract and pervasive pressure of knowing that for every ten metres you descend the weight of water above you increases by one atmosphere, and that at 3,100 metres you will be operating under three hundred and eleven atmospheres of pressure, and that the only thing standing between you and that pressure is 35 millimetres of borosilicate glass and a titanium frame and Stig's fourteen years of not dying.

The epipelagic zone — the sunlit zone, the top two hundred metres — took twelve minutes to pass through. This surprised me, as it always did. From the surface the ocean's depth is conceptually simple: you imagine it, as a vertical distance, and the imagination runs from here to there in an instant. But descending it in real time, at a rate of roughly sixteen metres per minute, gives it a physical reality that the imagination doesn't prepare you for. Twelve minutes to leave the sunlit world. At a hundred metres the light was already attenuated, the hammered pewter of the surface reduced to a faint luminosity above us. At a hundred and fifty it was the blue of deep dusk, the blue that has no reference on land. At two hundred it was gone.

"Mesopelagic," I said, for the log.

Stig acknowledged. Reyes made a note.

The mesopelagic — two hundred to a thousand metres — is the twilight zone, which is a name that sells it short. It is not twilight. It is the zone where light fails progressively and irrecoverably and where the biology of the ocean adapts to that failure in extraordinary ways. Here the bioluminescent organisms begin: the lanternfish with their rows of photophores, the siphonophores trailing their specialised cells, the copepods that produce light from their own bodies to communicate or attract or confuse. We passed through a layer of them in the first two hundred metres of the mesopelagic — a diffuse shimmer visible through the viewport, organisms so small they were individually invisible but collectively luminous, a curtain of cold fire that the DSV's forward motion disturbed and then left behind.

I watched it until it was gone.

Reyes said nothing. He was watching the instrument panel, which showed depth, pressure, internal atmosphere, external temperature, the passive acoustic array, the navigation feed from the surface. He had a specific quality of attention while reading instruments that was very like his quality of attention reading documents — total and outwardly still. I found, in those early minutes of the descent, that his stillness was useful. There was a version of this descent in which I might have talked too much, filling the silence with data, narrating what I saw in the precise compulsive way that I sometimes narrated when I was managing something that required management. His stillness made that unnecessary.

"Bathypelagic in thirty minutes," Stig said.

* * *

At six hundred metres the temperature dropped sharply through the thermocline, the boundary layer where the warm surface water met the cold deep. On the external temperature display the reading fell from twelve degrees to four in less than fifty metres of descent. The water changed colour with it — or rather, the colour we had been seeing, which was in any case the colour our external lights made in the water, shifted toward a deeper blue, a blue that was beginning to approach something other than blue entirely.

Reyes said: "Seven hundred."

"I see it."

At seven hundred metres we entered a marine snow layer — the constant slow fall of organic particles from the surface, the dead and dying and shed material of the upper ocean descending in a perpetual slow rain toward the seafloor. Seen through the viewport it was exactly what it sounded like: snow, but moving in all directions simultaneously, disturbed by the DSV's passage and by the minute currents of the deep, spiralling and drifting in patterns that were hypnotic and slightly vertiginous if you watched them too long.

I did not watch them too long.

A thousand metres. The mesopelagic ended and the bathypelagic began and this transition, unlike the one above, was not marked by light — because there was no light left to lose — but by something else, something that I had experienced on previous dives and never found quite the right word for. A quality of the dark. Above a thousand metres the dark, however complete, had always felt like an absence — the absence of light, which was a thing you knew existed somewhere above you. Below a thousand metres the dark became a presence. It had weight. It had texture. You could not see the texture but you knew it was there in the same way you knew the pressure was there: not through any single sense but through an accumulation of data from all of them, the body's whole repertoire of perception registering a new kind of environment.

"Bathypelagic," I said.

Stig acknowledged.

Reyes wrote the time in his log.

* * *

The descent from a thousand to three thousand metres took two hours. This was the longest part, and in some ways the strangest, because there was nothing to see except what the external lights showed — a small sphere of illuminated water around us, beyond which was absolute dark, and within which there was almost nothing except the occasional organism that crossed our path and was gone before I could fully register it. A brief silver flash that might have been a fish. Something gelatinous, translucent, trailing a filament, present for three seconds and then past the edge of the light. The marine snow, which had been heavier in the upper bathypelagic, thinning now to almost nothing.

Stig played music on his personal system. Something Scandinavian I didn't recognise, folk instrumentation, low volume. It was the right choice. The alternative was silence, and the silence down here was already doing something to all three of us that it was better not to amplify.

I checked the acoustic array. Since we'd entered the bathypelagic I had been running the passive array at low sensitivity, watching the same frequency range I'd been watching for months on every survey. Nothing. Background noise — the standard acoustic profile of deep Norwegian Sea water, the geology's low groan, the absence of shipping, the absence of biology. Clean.

I noted this. I noted it again at fifteen hundred metres.

"Two thousand," Reyes said.

I noted it again at twenty-five hundred.

At twenty-five hundred metres, Stig said: "Approaching target depth range. Three thousand in forty minutes."

"Good," Reyes said.

I looked at the acoustic display. Still clean. I thought: either the signal only propagates in certain conditions, or it only responds to specific stimuli and is otherwise silent, or we are not yet close enough to its source to detect it passively.

I thought: or it knows we're here and it's waiting.

I did not write that in the log.

* * *

At 2,800 metres, the noise stopped.

Not faded. Not attenuated. Stopped.

The acoustic array was running, the display was active, the system was functioning normally — all of this I checked in the two seconds after it happened, because the first thing I thought was equipment failure. It was not equipment failure. The passive array was receiving no signal at all in the frequency range I was monitoring, and then it was receiving no signal in any frequency range, and when I widened the display to show the full acoustic spectrum I saw that the array was returning a flat line across the board. No shipping rumble. No geological background. No biological scatter. The ocean, which is never acoustically silent because something is always producing sound somewhere, had simply stopped.

I said: "Reyes."

"I see it," he said. He had the acoustic log open on the instrument panel. The flat line was there too. He looked at it for a moment, then made a note in his log. The note said, I saw later when I read it: 2,800m. Ambient acoustic signature: zero. All frequencies. Duration: ongoing.

Stig had noticed. He was looking at his own instruments, his expression still, doing the same rapid fault-check I'd done. He said: "Systems are normal. The array is functional." A pause. "There's just nothing there."

We descended. The flat line held.

Nobody spoke for several minutes. The music had stopped — Stig had turned it off, though I hadn't noticed him doing it. The only sounds were the DSV's thrusters, which were barely audible at this speed, and the faint hiss of the life-support system, and our own breathing.

I looked out through the viewport. Dark. The external lights showed nothing but water and their own thin refraction in it. No organisms this deep. No marine snow. No movement.

Something had turned the ocean off.

Or the ocean — I corrected myself, in the specific way I corrected myself when I was edging toward a conclusion the data didn't yet support — the local acoustic environment had changed in a way that was consistent with being in a location where ambient sound was being absorbed or blocked or redirected by something I didn't yet understand. That was the accurate statement. The other statement was a category error. The ocean didn't turn off. The ocean had no intent.

I looked at the flat line on the display and thought about intent, and about recognition, and about four years of responses to our calibration pings, and I decided that I was going to hold the question of intent very carefully at the edge of my thinking and not let it move to the centre until I had evidence that required it there.

Reyes hadn't spoken. I glanced at him. He was looking at the acoustic display with the specific expression I was coming to recognise as his processing face — a quality of complete focus that was almost blank on the surface and was doing a great deal underneath.

I said, quietly: "It's like a door."

He looked at me.

"The silence," I said. "It doesn't feel like nothing. It feels like something."

He was quiet for a moment. Then he said: "Yes." Just that, and he went back to the instruments.

We continued down. The flat line held for the rest of the descent. Whatever was below us had drawn a boundary at 2,800 metres, and we had crossed it, and behind us the ordinary acoustic world of the Norwegian Sea continued its ordinary acoustic life without us.

We were in something else's territory now.

Neither of us said this aloud. Neither of us needed to.

* * *

At 2,800 metres, Stig brought the descent rate down to eight metres per minute. Standard practice when approaching survey depth in complex terrain — the Mohns Ridge here was heavily featured, the seafloor irregular, and coming in fast was how you encountered things you hadn't expected.

The external lights showed the first glimpse of the bottom at 3,050 metres: a dark surface resolving from the general dark, the kind of resolution that was more felt than seen at first, a texture emerging from the uniform black. Sediment. Fine-grained, pale grey in the lights, undisturbed. The geological record of the Norwegian Sea, layer on layer, going back further than anything human.

"Three hundred metres from survey coordinates," Stig said.

I checked the acoustic display. Flat line. I checked it again. Still flat.

I looked at the seafloor and thought about the coordinates — 73.17 degrees North, 11.43 degrees East, 3,100 metres — where the Aurora Seven had last been logged, and where there was, according to every sonar survey conducted since, no trace of a 14,000-tonne semi-submersible rig or its twenty-four crew.

"Coming up on coordinates," Stig said.

I looked out the viewport at the undisturbed sediment and the absolute dark beyond our lights and said nothing.

We were here.

ELEVEN

The Rig

There was nothing at the coordinates.

We held position at 3,100 metres, the DSV hovering on its thrusters three metres above the seafloor, and the external lights showed us pale grey sediment in every direction, undisturbed, featureless, the flat geological record of the Norwegian Sea extending to the edge of our visibility and presumably beyond. No wreckage. No debris field. No structural components scattered by an implosion or distributed by currents. The seafloor at 73.17 North, 11.43 East was exactly what the sonar surveys had said it was: empty.

I noted the time. I noted the acoustic display, which was still flat. I noted the external temperature — 1.8 degrees, consistent with deep Norwegian Sea water, no anomalous thermal gradient. I noted the sediment character as far as the lights allowed: undisturbed, uniform, no unusual formations in the immediate vicinity.

I had expected nothing and I was still somehow surprised by nothing. There is a difference between knowing a thing intellectually and being three kilometres underwater looking at the absence of a structure that weighed 14,000 tonnes and housed twenty-four people and realising that the absence is complete, clean, total — not the absence of something that was destroyed, which leaves its own particular kind of evidence, but the absence of something that was simply no longer where it had been.

"No debris," Stig said. He said it the way he said most things: factually, without inflection. He had logged the observation.

"No debris," Reyes confirmed. He was looking at the sonar display, which showed the seafloor topography in a hundred-metre radius —

flat, flat, slightly elevated near what the charts said was the ridge wall two hundred metres to the east.

I looked out the viewport. Sediment. Dark. Our four lights making their small bright claim on the bottom of the Norwegian Sea.

Reyes said: "I want to expand the search radius."

"The sonar surveys covered two kilometres," I said.

"I know." He was still looking at the display. "I want to go to 3.2 kilometres. Bearing zero-four-seven."

I said: "Why zero-four-seven?"

He was quiet for a moment. Then he said: "Because the rig's last station-keeping adjustment, eleven hours before it went dark, was a one-degree heading correction to zero-four-seven. It was logged as routine. I think it wasn't routine."

I looked at him. He was still looking at the display, his expression unreadable.

"Stig," he said, "bearing zero-four-seven, three-point-two kilometres from current position. Slow approach."

"Understood," Stig said, and we moved.

* * *

The transit took nine minutes. We travelled three metres above the seafloor, the lights showing us the sediment scrolling past, occasional geological features resolving from the dark and passing behind us — a ridge of consolidated basalt, a small canyon, the exposed edge of a sediment layer that had been undercut by some ancient current and now projected slightly into the water column. Standard deep-ridge terrain. Nothing anomalous. The acoustic display remained flat.

At three kilometres, Stig said: "Something on the sonar."

He did not say what the something was. He did not need to. On the navigation sonar display, at the edge of the effective range, there was a return — a solid, large-scale return, the kind that meant something substantial on the seafloor ahead of us. The kind that a 14,000-tonne structure would produce if it were intact and sitting on the bottom.

Nobody said anything. Stig slowed our approach to two metres per minute. I watched the sonar return grow in resolution as we closed the distance, the shape of it emerging: not the scattered pattern of debris, not the irregular topology of a geological feature, but a regular outline, roughly rectangular, with projecting structures at the corners and along the sides that resolved as we drew closer into the specific configuration of a semi-submersible drilling rig's pontoon and column arrangement.

I knew that configuration. I had looked at the Aurora Seven's engineering specifications for three weeks. I knew the shape of her.

"Three-point-two kilometres from original coordinates," Stig said. "Target consistent with large structural object. Class four semi-submersible configuration." He paused. "Intact."

We came around a low ridge and she was there.

* * *

The Aurora Seven sat on the seafloor of the Norwegian Sea as though she had always been there, and the wrongness of this was total and immediate and required no analysis.

She was intact. Not damaged-but-recognisable, not partially collapsed, not resting on her side. She was upright, level, her four corner columns standing vertical, her upper deck approximately forty metres above the seafloor, her drill tower still in place. Eighty-five days after disappearing from every sensor and search operation that had looked for her, she was sitting on the bottom of the Norwegian Sea in the same operational configuration she had been in when she went dark.

Stig brought us to a stop fifteen metres from her hull. The DSV's lights illuminated the nearest column from deck level to seafloor. The paint was intact. The external cabling was in place. The equipment housing on the near column — a sensor cluster that should have been destroyed by any implosion energetic enough to take the rig to the bottom in minutes — was undamaged.

"She's intact," Reyes said. He was not saying it to report. He was saying it the way you say something that you need to hear in your own voice before you can fully believe it.

"Yes," I said.

"The hull integrity looks uncompromised. The structural members are in place. The drill tower." He said this last word as though it were a specific impossibility. The drill tower of a semi-submersible, in an uncontrolled descent, generates enormous hydrodynamic forces. The tower should have been the first thing to fail.

"She didn't fall," I said. I said it as I understood it, which was in the same moment I said it. "She was placed."

Stig, who had not spoken since identifying the target, said nothing.

Reyes said: "Take us around her. Full circuit. All lights."

* * *

We circled the Aurora Seven at a distance of ten metres. Stig took us slowly — one full circuit at deck level, one at mid-column height, one at pontoon level — and I recorded everything: exterior video from the DSV's cameras, my own narration for the log, Reyes's instrument readings. The circuit took forty-seven minutes.

The rig was undamaged. Not superficially undamaged — structurally undamaged. The welds were intact. The external piping was connected. The satellite antenna array on the upper deck was in place, its dishes in the stowed position they would have been in during operational mode. We found no impact marks on the hull, no crushing or buckling consistent with an uncontrolled descent through 3,100 metres of water, no evidence of any event violent enough to be called a catastrophic structural failure.

The hatches were sealed.

All of them. Every external access point on the Aurora Seven — eight main hatches, four emergency exits, the two equipment airlocks on the lower deck — was sealed closed. Not just dogged shut, which was their normal operational state. Sealed. The hatch surfaces, when we moved close enough for the lights to resolve the detail, showed a material covering the seam line that our external chemical sensors read as organic in composition and unknown in specific type. It was dark, almost black, smooth, and continuous — it followed the hatch seams precisely, as though it had been applied with knowledge of where the seams were. It had hardened. The sensors gave no temperature differential between the material and the surrounding steel.

"What is that," I said. It was not a question. It was the noise a person makes when their vocabulary hasn't yet caught up with what they're looking at.

Reyes said: "Unknown." He was recording the chemical sensor readings. "Organic matrix, carbon-based, structural integrity suggesting it's been there at least several weeks. Nothing in the database."

"It's sealing them in," I said.

"Or sealing other things out."

I looked at the nearest hatch and thought about twenty-four people on the other side of it, and then I thought about whether thinking about twenty-four people on the other side of it was something I was able to sustain, and I decided that I could sustain it as long as I kept moving, kept recording, kept the professional part of my attention in the foreground.

"No bodies," I said. "External surfaces are clear."

"No bodies," Reyes confirmed.

"If there had been an implosion —"

"There wasn't an implosion."

"No."

We finished the circuit.

* * *

It was Stig who found the porthole.

He had brought us back to the upper deck level, moving slowly along the accommodation block — the section of the rig where the crew quarters were located, a section I had been specifically trying not to look at too directly. The accommodation block had twelve portholes on its eastern face, spaced at two-metre intervals. Stig was running the lights across them in sequence, systematically, the way he did everything.

At the seventh porthole from the southern end, he stopped.

"Light," he said.

Through the porthole, visible against the dark interior of the accommodation block, there was a light. Not our own lights reflected in the glass — a light from inside, warm in colour, the specific warm colour of a cabin reading lamp or a corridor emergency light. A small rectangle of amber in all that black.

"Someone's inside," Reyes said.

The word someone landed in the sphere with a weight that the word rig had not, because rig was a structure and someone was a person and persons were different from structures in all the ways that mattered most right now. I looked at the porthole and I thought: there is a person on the other side of that glass. In a rig that has been sitting on the bottom of the Norwegian Sea for eighty-five days. In a rig with sealed hatches. A person with a light on.

Stig moved us closer. We came to within two metres of the porthole and held position there, the DSV's lights angled to illuminate the exterior without flooding the interior, and through the glass we could see the interior of a crew cabin: a bunk on the far wall, a small desk, a door standing open to a corridor beyond. And at the desk, their back to us, seated in the chair with the specific stillness of someone who had been sitting for a long time — a person.

A person in coveralls. Short-haired. Both hands on the desk surface, palms down. Sitting very still.

"Hello," Stig said. He said it quietly, reflexively, the way you greet someone before you've fully registered that greeting them is absurd given the circumstances. He immediately looked slightly embarrassed about having said it. Neither Reyes nor I commented.

Reyes reached for the communications panel and keyed the external speakers — the DSV had an underwater communications system, designed for diver support, that could project sound into the water outside the hull. He said: "Aurora Seven crew, this is a rescue vessel. If you can hear me, please face the porthole."

The person at the desk did not move.

He repeated it. Three times, in English, then twice in Norwegian. The person at the desk remained as they were — hands on the surface, back to the porthole, still.

"They may not be able to hear us," I said. "The acoustic insulation in the hull"

"Or they can't respond," Reyes said.

"Or they're —" I stopped.

"No," Reyes said. "Look at the posture. That's not someone who's dead. That's someone who's sitting."

He was right. The person at the desk had the posture of someone at rest, not the posture of someone who had died in a chair. Their head was upright. Their hands were arranged, not fallen.

They were alive. At three thousand and one hundred metres depth, in a sealed rig that had been on the bottom of the Norwegian Sea for eighty-five days, a person was sitting at a desk with their hands flat on the surface and their back to the porthole and a reading lamp on, and they were alive.

I put my hand against the viewport. It was a thing I did without deciding to do it — the body's impulse, the thing the hand does when you cannot cross the distance between yourself and someone on the other side of a barrier. The glass was cold. The person at the desk did not turn around.

I pressed my palm flat against it and held it there and looked at the back of their head through metres of water and the glass of a submersible viewport and the glass of a cabin porthole, and I did not know their name, and I did not know what had happened to them, and I did not know what was going to happen next.

I knew one thing, which was that they were alive, and that alive was not what they were supposed to be, and that everything I had thought I was prepared for when Reyes said we need to go down there had not included this.

Behind us, in the dark and the silence and the cold, the Aurora Seven sat on the seafloor with her lights on and her hatches sealed and twenty-four people inside her, and whatever had put her there was not anywhere we could see.

TWELVE

The Structure

Reyes was the one who pulled me away from the porthole.

He didn't touch me. He said my name, once, in the even tone he used for operational instructions, and I removed my hand from the glass and turned around and he was looking at me in the way he looked at things that required careful handling. I was not going to apologise for the moment at the porthole. He was not going to ask me to.

"We need to survey the immediate area," he said. "Before we do anything else, I need to know what we're sitting in."

This was correct. This was the right next action. I was grateful for it.

"Agreed," I said.

Stig, who had been holding position at the accommodation block, moved us back to the eastern face of the rig and then south, expanding our survey radius in the direction of the ridge wall. The acoustic display was still flat. The external temperature was still 1.8 degrees. The external lights showed the seafloor in a moving circle of pale grey that resolved into whatever was ahead of us and dissolved back into dark behind.

For the first hundred metres south of the Aurora Seven there was nothing: undisturbed sediment, the same featureless geological floor we'd seen at the original coordinates. I watched it and kept the recording systems running and said nothing because there was nothing to say yet.

At a hundred and twelve metres, the sediment changed.

* * *

It took me a moment to understand what I was seeing, and then another moment after that to be certain I was seeing it correctly, because what I was seeing required a specific kind of looking — the kind that had to first discard the assumption that it was natural, which was the assumption you brought to the deep seafloor because the deep seafloor was always natural, and then look again with the assumption removed.

The sediment surface, which had been flat and uniform, now showed texture. But not the texture of geological process — not the ripple patterns of bottom currents, not the irregular hummocking of accumulated organic material, not the surface expression of buried gas structures. This was a different kind of texture. It rose in low regular forms from the seafloor, forms that were only a few centimetres proud of the surrounding sediment but were distributed in a pattern that repeated: a row of slightly elevated ovoids, each approximately half a metre in its longest dimension, spaced at consistent intervals. Then a gap. Then another row, offset from the first by half an interval. Then another gap. Then another row.

"Stop," I said.

Stig stopped.

I looked at the pattern. My brain was trying to classify it — trying to fit it into a category from the taxonomy of seafloor features I had spent twelve years developing and refining — and the taxonomy was not cooperating. The forms were not geological. The regularity was not biological. The spacing was not random.

I said: "Can you take us lower? Two metres above the surface. And slow."

Stig brought us down and we moved forward at walking speed and I watched the pattern come under us and pass behind us. The ovoids were arranged in offset rows extending as far as our lights could resolve — which was perhaps forty metres in each direction at this altitude, beyond which they faded into the dark. The interval between the forms within a row was consistent to a degree that I would have called, in any data context, mathematically regular.

"This isn't geological," I said.

"No," Reyes said.

"Or biological. Nothing biological produces this kind of spatial regularity at this scale."

"No," he said again.

We looked at it together. Below us the pattern continued, row after offset row, extending south toward the ridge wall and — when Stig turned us to check — north as well, the rig rising from it in the middle distance like something built into it rather than resting on top of it.

* * *

We spent an hour surveying the area around the rig. The pattern of forms was not uniform across the whole space — in some sections the rows were denser, the ovoids more pronounced, the distribution more complex. In other sections the forms were barely visible, mere suggestions of regularity in the sediment surface, easily dismissed as natural variation if you were looking at sonar data from a vessel rather than lights through a viewport two metres above the bottom.

Easily dismissed. That phrase stayed with me. I thought about all the surveys that had passed over this location in the past four years. I thought about the sonar data I had reviewed and filed and certified, including the data from this exact location, and about whether this structure — if structure was the right word — would have been visible in that data, and I concluded that at standard survey resolution it would not have been. The forms were too low, the sediment contrast too slight. They would have resolved as sediment texture variation, which was standard, which was background, which was not worth noting.

I thought: twelve years. I thought: how long has this been here.

The answer to that question was not available to me at this moment. What was available to me was the camera feed and the instrument readings and the specific quality of light the external systems threw across the forms when we were at the right angle — a raking light that revealed edges and shadows invisible at other angles — and the specific quality of the surfaces when we came close enough for the lights to resolve them at high detail.

The surfaces were wrong.

Not wrong in the way that you described an incorrect measurement or a violated expectation. Wrong in the way that a thing looked when it was made by a process you did not recognise and could not reverse-engineer from the result. The ovoid forms were not the random product of sedimentation or geological pressure. Their surfaces were smooth in a way that sediment-derived structures were not smooth — not polished, not glassy, but consistently, uniformly smooth, the way the surface of a bone was smooth, or the shell of a deep-sea organism, or the outside of something that had grown slowly in one direction for a very long time.

"Reyes," I said.

"I see it."

"The surface texture. It's consistent with biogenic —"

"Don't classify it yet," he said. Quietly but precisely. "Not out loud."

I stopped. I understood what he meant: once you said a word for it, the word became the first data point in every analysis that followed, and in this context the word you chose — the first word, the framing word — would matter in ways neither of us could yet assess. I had been about to say biogenic, which meant produced by living organisms, and I had been about to say it because it was accurate, and Reyes was right that saying it out loud, here, on a recording that would be reviewed by people who had sent him on a maritime safety audit, was premature.

"Understood," I said.

We continued surveying. The structure — I was using the word in my head now, unavoidably — extended at least two hundred metres in each direction from the rig. We did not find its edge before Reyes said we needed to stop.

* * *

"We need to ascend," Reyes said.

It was the first time he had suggested it and I had known it was coming. I said: "We haven't completed the documentation."

"We have footage and instrument data from the survey area. We have visual confirmation of the rig. We have enough to report."

"We have enough to report what we've seen," I said. "We don't have enough to explain it. We don't have species identification on the surface material. We don't have depth mapping of the structure's extent. We don't have —"

"Mara."

"We came down here to find out what was here. We've found something. We should document it before we leave."

"We've been down for four hours and twenty minutes," he said. "We have a seven-hour operational window. If we stay and complete a full documentation sweep we come up with a thirty-minute buffer. If anything goes wrong on the ascent —"

"Nothing's going to go wrong on the ascent."

"You don't know that." He said it without heat. "Nobody knows that. That's the nature of a half-hour buffer."

I looked at the display, which showed the structure extending beyond our lights in every direction. I looked at the rig, still visible to the north, the warm amber light of the porthole a small specific thing in all that dark.

"Twenty-four people," I said.

"Yes."

"We know they're alive. We know the hatches are sealed from the outside. We know whatever sealed them is organic and of unknown origin. We know this structure exists and extends at least two hundred metres around the rig in all directions. If we leave now with only what we have —"

"If we leave now we can report what we've found and come back with more time and better equipment and a plan for what we're going to do with what we find."

I looked at him. He looked back at me. He was not afraid. I was not afraid. We were two people with different ideas about what the data required and who had different institutional frameworks for deciding what happened next, and we were having that argument three kilometres underwater with a sealed rig behind us and a structure of unknown origin below us and an acoustic display that had shown a flat line for the past four hours.

"This is the best data we're going to get," I said. "Down here, now, with the lights on it. Once we ascend and report, whatever happens next doesn't look like a scientific survey anymore."

He was quiet for a moment.

"You don't trust what comes after," he said.

"I don't know what comes after. Neither do you. But I know what happens to data once it enters institutional channels before it's been properly characterised, and I know that the person best positioned to characterise it is on this submersible right now with cameras running."

Another silence. Stig was keeping us steady, looking at his instruments, doing a very professional job of not being present for this conversation.

Reyes said: "One hour. Then we ascend."

I said: "One hour."

He reached for the instrument panel and logged the extension. His entry said: Extended survey period approved. Scientific documentation of anomalous seafloor features. End time 12.40.

He did not say: you were right. Neither did I. We did not need to.

* * *

In the hour that followed I documented everything I could reach in the available time. I ran the spectrometer on three separate sections of the ovoid forms — the readings were consistent across all three: carbon-based, complex organic matrix, no mineral substrate, a specific density profile that the onboard database could not match to any known deep-sea organism or biogenic structure. I photographed the surface texture at high resolution from eight different angles and with four different lighting configurations. I measured the spacing between forms in six separate rows and found the interval variation was less than two percent — less than the measurement tolerance of the instruments, which meant it was either exactly regular or regular to a degree my equipment could not resolve.

I noted all of this. I did not say it out loud.

What I thought, while I was doing it, was this: something built this. Not assembled it, not arranged it — those words were too deliberate, too mechanical, too human. Something grew this. Something that had been here, at 3,100 metres, on this section of the Mohns Ridge, for long enough to produce a structure that extended at least two hundred metres in radius from a central point that was, not coincidentally, the exact location where the Aurora Seven had been operating.

Something that had been producing acoustic signals for four years. Something that had arranged a 14,000-tonne rig on its seafloor with the internal lights still on. Something that had sealed twenty-four people inside it and kept them alive for eighty-five days at depth.

I did not write any of this in the log.

At 12.38 I finished the final instrument sweep and stowed the equipment and told Stig we were ready.

He initiated the ascent.

As we rose, I looked back through the viewport. The structure was visible as long as our external lights could reach it — the low forms in their offset rows, the sediment texture resolving back into uniform grey as the distance increased, the Aurora Seven growing smaller and then smaller again, the amber point of the porthole light holding longer than anything else, a warm specific dot diminishing in all that absolute dark until it was gone.

I kept looking for another few seconds after it disappeared. Then I turned back to the instruments and watched the depth display count upward and did not let myself think too far ahead.

Behind us, something moved in the structure. Unhurried. Purposeful.

A decision had been made.

THIRTEEN

Surface Interruption

The DSV had been in the water for three hours and fourteen minutes when Yuna found the structure in the data, and she almost missed it because she was looking for something else.

She had been working since the launch, which was how she worked: not starting when the project started, not starting when other people arrived, but starting earlier, in the gaps between official activity, in the private hours when the material was just her and the question and no institutional scaffolding around either. The Lofoten's data deck was quiet. Magnus was monitoring the support systems on the instrument side of the room, doing something with a software update that required occasional concentrated attention and nothing else. The hydrophone array was deployed. The passive acoustic monitoring was running. And Yuna was at her own workstation with the full archive of signal recordings — every detection, from the 2019 calibration response onward — open on three screens.

She had a specific project. Mara had given her the temporal mapping she'd run before departure — the analysis showing the interval drift, the fractional quickening of the pulse rhythm over four years — and Yuna had identified something in it that she wanted to pursue. Not the drift itself, which Mara had characterised correctly. Something adjacent to the drift, something in the relationship between the drift and the interval architecture, that she had a hypothesis about and had not yet said out loud.

The hypothesis required her to look at the full signal corpus not as acoustic data but as something else. This was the part that she was still working out how to do, because the tools she had were acoustic analysis tools, designed by and for people who were trying to characterise natural and anthropogenic sound sources, and she needed to use them to ask a question they had not been designed to answer.

What she needed to know was whether the pattern, across its full documented history, showed evidence of the thing that all organised communication systems showed: compression.

* * *

Compression was not a simple concept. In information theory it referred to the encoding of meaning in the most efficient possible form — the removal of redundancy, the maximisation of signal relative to noise, the packing of content into the minimum necessary structure. Every human language compressed. Every animal communication system that had been studied in sufficient detail compressed. The mathematics of compression were well understood; there were theorems, going back to Shannon in the mid-twentieth century, that described the fundamental limits of how efficiently information could be encoded in a signal of given properties.

The reason Yuna was thinking about compression was the two-to-one ratio.

She had been thinking about the two-to-one ratio since the first evening in Tromsø, when Mara had shown her the data and she had said, quietly, two to one, and written it inside her own head. The ratio was the most persistent feature of the signal across all its documented variations — it survived changes in duration, changes in intensity, the interval drift, the response to external stimuli. It was structural in the way that the frame of a sentence was structural: not the content, but the architecture that the content was arranged within.

In tonal language systems — the linguistic family that included Mandarin, Cantonese, Vietnamese, Yoruba, and several hundred other languages in which pitch and duration carried meaning at the level of the syllable rather than merely the level of stress — the mathematical relationship between tone durations was not arbitrary. It was constrained by compression principles. The ratios between tones in a tonal system tended to cluster around small integer relationships — two to one, three to two, four to three — because these ratios were computationally efficient: they were easy to generate, easy to distinguish, and easy to stack into more complex structures without exceeding the encoding capacity of the channel.

The two-to-one ratio was the simplest possible tonal duration relationship. It was also, across the world's tonal language systems, the most common.

Yuna had not said this to Mara. Not yet. She was still assembling the analysis that would let her say it with the precision it required.

* * *

The analysis took two hours and forty minutes. She ran the full corpus through three separate compression analyses, each using a different mathematical framework, and compared the results. What she was looking for was whether the signal's frequency distribution — the way different pulse durations and intervals were used across all documented detections — was consistent with an efficient encoding scheme or consistent with random variation within a fixed parameter set.

The distinction mattered. A signal that varied randomly within a fixed range was a signal that had range but no vocabulary. A signal that varied in ways consistent with compression — where certain configurations appeared more often than chance predicted, where rare configurations appeared in specific contexts rather than randomly, where the overall distribution of configurations approximated the efficiency limit described by information theory — was a signal that was doing something.

By the time the third analysis completed, Yuna had her answer.

The signal was not varying randomly. Its frequency distribution showed the specific skew of compressed information: a core of high-frequency configurations that appeared consistently across detections, a set of medium-frequency configurations that appeared in variable contexts, and a long tail of rare configurations that appeared, on closer examination, in conditions that differed systematically from the baseline. The skew matched — not perfectly, not conclusively, but within a range that would have constituted a publishable result in any of three journals she could name — the theoretical distribution predicted by

Shannon's source coding theorem for a communication system operating near its efficiency limit.

She sat back.

She had been in the field long enough to know the difference between a result that told you what you'd hoped to find and a result that told you something that required you to revise what you'd hoped to find entirely. This was the second kind. She had gone looking for compression and she had found compression, but finding it meant that the question was no longer whether the signal was organised. The question was now considerably more specific, and considerably harder.

She wrote in her notebook: Signal corpus shows frequency distribution consistent with compressed information encoding. Core vocabulary stable across four-year corpus. Long-tail configurations context-dependent. Efficiency approaching Shannon limit.

She looked at what she had written. Then she wrote below it, in smaller letters, the thing she had not yet said to anyone: This is not a signal. This is a language.

She closed the notebook. On the acoustic monitoring display, three metres from where she was sitting, the passive array's feed showed the ambient acoustic environment of the Norwegian Sea, which had been flat for hours. Mara and Reyes were three kilometres below her. They had gone down to find out what was there and they had not yet come back up.

Yuna thought: I need to tell Mara.

She thought: Mara is three kilometres underwater.

She thought: I will tell her when she surfaces.

She made tea.

* * *

An hour later, Magnus said: "There's a vessel on radar."

He said it the way he said most things — flatly, informatively, without assessment. He had pulled up the navigation display and was looking at it with the same mild professional attention he brought to every instrument reading.

Yuna went over to look.

The contact was at a distance of approximately eight kilometres, bearing two-seven-zero. It was moving slowly, perhaps four knots, in what appeared to be a holding pattern — not a direct transit course, not a fishing vessel's working pattern, but a slow wide circle that kept it at a consistent distance from the Lofoten's position.

"AIS?" Yuna said.

"No AIS signal."

She looked at the contact. Eight kilometres was well outside visual range. The radar signature was consistent with a vessel in the 30-to-50-metre range — not a small craft, not a commercial ship. She watched it for two minutes. Its course was a consistent arc, the distance to the Lofoten varying by less than half a kilometre across the full observable portion of the arc.

"It's circling us," she said.

"Yes," Magnus said, with the tone of someone who had reached the same conclusion thirty seconds earlier and had been waiting for confirmation.

She keyed the communications panel and switched to the encrypted channel Reyes had established before the dive. "Reyes, this is surface. We have an unregistered vessel at eight kilometres, bearing two-seven-zero, running without AIS. Appears to be holding a surveillance position. Please advise."

There was a delay of nearly a minute — she knew they were deep enough that the communications lag was significant, the signal routing through the acoustic modem at the DSV's upper end. Then Reyes's voice came back, slightly compressed by the encoding: "Copy that. Log the contact. Bearing, speed, estimated size. Do not attempt to hail or establish contact. Continue current operations."

She logged it. She continued current operations.

But she watched the contact for the next forty minutes, until it changed its arc to a departure course and disappeared from radar, and she thought about Reyes's response. She had given him information about an unidentified vessel conducting what looked like surveillance of their position, and he had told her to log it and not react.

Not: I don't know what that is.

Not: That's unusual.

Not: Keep an eye on it.

He had told her not to hail it. Which meant he had an opinion about what would happen if she did. Which meant he knew, or suspected he knew, what it was.

She looked at the blank radar display where the contact had been and thought about what kind of vessel ran without AIS and conducted surveillance patterns at eight kilometres range and was not, apparently, a surprise to a US Navy officer running a deep-sea investigation in Norwegian waters.

She thought: someone else is watching.

She thought: Reyes already knew that was possible.

She thought: he didn't tell Mara.

She wrote none of this in the log. She went back to her workstation, to the signal corpus and its compressed vocabulary and the thing she had not yet said out loud. On the acoustic monitoring display the passive array continued its flat recording. Below her, somewhere in the dark, Mara was in a pressure sphere at 3,100 metres, and whatever had been answering their signals for four years was somewhere close to her.

Yuna checked the communications panel. Still connected. She looked at the data. She waited.

* * *

The DSV surfaced at 15.22. Yuna was on the aft deck when the crane brought it out of the water. The sphere broke the surface and the Norwegian Sea ran off it in sheets and Stig was first out of the hatch, then Reyes, then Mara, who stood at the top of the access ladder for a moment looking at the horizon as though she needed to confirm it was still there.

Yuna let Reyes debrief first with the Lofoten's navigator and the watch officer, the operational necessities, the things that had to happen before anything else. She stood near the aft rail and watched the sea and waited.

When Mara came to her she looked the way she had looked in Tromsø when Yuna had told her she looked terrible: not poorly but fully occupied, as though something very large was taking up most of the space inside her and there was not much room left for the surface presentation of composure.

Yuna said: "The vessel went away."

"What vessel?"

"Unregistered. Running without AIS. Held a surveillance position at eight kilometres for about forty minutes, then left. I reported it to Reyes."

Mara looked at her. "What did he say?"

"Log it and don't hail it."

A pause. Mara looked toward Reyes, who was completing his debrief twenty metres away, and then back at Yuna. Something crossed her face that was not quite surprise and not quite recognition but was in the territory between them. "He knew what it was," she said.

"That's what I thought."

"He didn't say anything to me." She said it not as an accusation — more as a data point, something to be filed and returned to.

"No," Yuna said. "He didn't."

They stood for a moment in the particular silence of two people who have each found something that day that they need to tell the other, and who are not quite sure which thing to say first.

Mara said: "There's a rig down there. Intact. Crew inside."

Yuna held this for a moment. "Alive?"

"Yes."

"And the structure? The thing in the data?"

"Real. Larger than I thought. We didn't find the edge of it."

Yuna nodded slowly. She looked at the water.

"I found something too," she said. "While you were down. I need to show you the analysis. But not here."

"Tonight," Mara said.

"Tonight."

The sea moved around them, grey and comprehensive, and somewhere below it the Aurora Seven sat with its lights on and its hatches sealed, and the structure extended outward from it in all directions into the dark, and eight kilometres to the west a vessel without a name was heading back toward wherever it had come from, carrying whatever it had seen.

FOURTEEN

The Touch

We went down again the following morning.

The decision had been made the night before, in the analysis room, after Yuna showed us what she'd found. She had put the frequency distribution on the primary screen and walked us through the compression analysis in the precise, economical way she explained things — no dramatization, no hedging, just the mathematics and what the mathematics indicated. Reyes had asked four questions, all technical, all answered. I had asked none, because I had seen where she was going from the first chart and had needed the silence to sit in it.

When she finished, she had said: the signal corpus shows a frequency distribution consistent with compressed information encoding, approaching the theoretical efficiency limit for a communication system operating in this channel. And then, quietly: I think this is a language.

The three of us had sat with that for a while in the specific way that you sit with something that reorganises everything around it.

Reyes had said, finally: then we need a second pass. With the acoustic emitter.

I had known he would say it. I had known before he said it that I agreed, and that agreeing would mean going back down into the dark to what we had found — the rig, the structure, the person sitting at the desk who had not turned around — and this time not just observing. Responding. Sending something back into the channel and waiting to see what the channel returned.

We had gone to bed. In the morning we had gone back into the water.

* * *

The second descent was different from the first in the way that all returns are different: the strangeness was still there, but it had a known shape now, and knowing the shape changed it. The transition through the zones — the dying light, the bioluminescent curtain, the deepening dark, the thermocline — we moved through quickly, not rushing the descent rate but not lingering. Stig kept the music off from the start this time.

The silence came at 2,800 metres, as before. The flat line on the acoustic display. The complete cessation of ambient noise across all frequencies, as though we had crossed a threshold into a different kind of water.

As though we had come back.

"2,800," Reyes said. He noted it in the log.

"Same position as yesterday," I said.

He nodded. We descended.

At 2,600 metres I had checked the passive acoustic array. Normal ambient profile — the Norwegian Sea's standard background. At 2,800 I checked it again. Flat, as expected. At 3,000 I checked it a third time and held the display open in front of me and watched it.

We reached survey depth at 09.47 and Stig held position above the structure while I ran a systems check on the active emitter. The emitter was the DSV's onboard sonar — a low-frequency unit designed for seafloor mapping, not the kind of active sonar used for detection or communication. It was capable of producing pulses in the calibration frequency range I needed. I had spent an hour the previous evening configuring the pulse parameters: the frequency, the duration, the interval structure. The inversion.

I had memorised the sequence from the original 2019 calibration data. The calibration had used a sweep of six frequency components at the two-to-one interval. I had configured the emitter to produce the same six components in reverse order, at the same interval. Inverted.

"Systems ready," I said.

"Understood," Reyes said. He had his log open. The instrument panel showed depth, pressure, battery status, external temperature. All normal. The passive acoustic array: flat.

"We wait first," I said. "I want to know what's here before I transmit."

"Agreed."

We held position. Stig kept us steady above the structure. The external lights showed the low ovoid forms below us, the offset rows extending into the dark.

We waited for twenty minutes and nothing changed. The acoustic display stayed flat. The structure was still. The lights outside were steady. The DSV hovered on its thrusters and the Norwegian Sea sat on top of us and three kilometres above that the Lofoten sat on the surface of the world with Yuna at her hydrophone array and Magnus at his instruments, and everything was still.

I activated the emitter.

* * *

The pulse lasted 83 seconds. Six components, reversed, at the two-to-one interval. I watched the acoustic display as it went out — the active emitter's output visible as a separate channel, the pulse moving away from us in all directions at the speed of sound through cold water. I counted. The pulse completed. The emitter went silent. The display returned to passive mode.

Flat.

Twenty seconds. Thirty. I watched the passive channel and Reyes watched the instruments and Stig watched everything and the structure below us was still.

At thirty-seven seconds — exactly thirty-seven seconds, which was the duration of a single sequence — the lights went out.

Not all the way. Not darkness. The external lights dimmed, from full operational brightness to perhaps forty percent, in a smooth controlled reduction, the kind of reduction that a rheostat produced when you turned it, not the kind that a power failure produced. The kind that was deliberate. The instruments showed no fault in the power system. The batteries were at full charge. The lights had dimmed because something had dimmed them.

"Power draw anomaly," Reyes said, very quietly.

"Not a fault," I said.

"No."

In the reduced light the structure below us had a different quality — the shadows between the ovoid forms were deeper now, the forms themselves sharper in relief, the geometry more apparent. I looked at it and then looked away and looked at the passive acoustic display, which was still flat, and then I felt it.

Not heard. Felt. The distinction was real and important: the sequence arrived not through my ears but through the hull of the DSV, transmitted through the pressure sphere's titanium frame and the glass and my seat and my spine. A vibration. Very low frequency, below the threshold of normal hearing, in the range that the body registered as physical rather than acoustic — the range of standing in front of a large speaker, or near a running engine, or at the edge of a storm. The range of bass that you felt in your sternum.

The sequence. Six pulses, the familiar interval structure, the two-to-one ratio. The same pattern I had been studying for months, had been trying to characterise and explain and contextualise within every available framework and had failed to fit in any of them. Here, now, transmitted through the structure and the water and the metal of the sphere and into my body, it was immediate in a way that data had never been.

"It's transmitting," Reyes said. His voice was level. His eyes were on the passive acoustic display, which was now showing signal — the pattern visible as a clean regular series of spikes against the flat baseline, exactly as it had appeared in the survey data, except that the survey data had been recorded at a distance and this was being recorded from a position approximately ten metres above its source.

"It heard us," I said.

"Yes."

The sequence ran to completion. Eighty-three seconds. Six pulses, the long pause, six pulses. Silence.

The lights were still at forty percent.

I looked at the emitter controls.

* * *

I want to describe what I was thinking in the moment before I reached for the emitter, and the honest answer is that I am not certain thinking is the right word. There was something happening that was less deliberate than thinking and more deliberate than instinct — a recognition, a pattern-match, something that had been building for months and arrived in that moment as a completed circuit. I had sent the inverted sequence. It had received the inverted sequence. It had replied with the original. We were in an exchange. We were in a call and response. We were in something that had the structure, if Yuna was right, of communication.

And the right response to communication, when you receive it, is to respond.

I reached forward and activated the emitter and sent the inverted sequence again. The same six components, the same reversal, the same interval. I sent it and took my hand off the control and waited.

The thirty-seven-second interval passed. Eighty-three seconds. The passive display was still showing the previous detection, fading back to baseline.

And then something happened to the lights.

* * *

It began at the edge of our illuminated circle, at the perimeter where the external lights met the dark and gave way to it. A faint luminescence — not our lights reflected back, not an instrument artifact, but a genuine emission from something in the water outside the DSV. Cold blue-green, the specific colour of deep-sea bioluminescence, which is not the warm yellow of incandescent light or the white of fluorescent but something older and more specific: the colour that living things make in the dark when they need to be seen.

It was moving.

I watched it move and I did not speak and I did not look away. It came from the edge of our light circle toward the DSV in a way that was not the movement of a current — not passive, not drifting, but directed. It moved along the hull of the DSV, from the nose back toward the thruster array, following the line of the frame, the shape of the vehicle. Not surrounding us. Tracing us.

"It's outlining us," Reyes said. He said it the way you said a fact when the fact was what your mind had available. His voice was completely steady. I did not know how his voice was completely steady. Mine would not have been if I had tried to speak.

The bioluminescence continued along the hull. It found the thruster array and moved around it and came back along the other side, following the exact contour of the frame, the cold light distributed not as a glow but as a line — a precise tracing of the DSV's outline, as though something was examining the shape of us and making a record of it in light.

It reached the front of the vehicle and the viewport and stopped.

And held.

The cold blue-green light sat at the forward edge of the DSV, perhaps half a metre from the glass, distributed across a section of water that had no shape we could identify — nothing resolved into a body or a form, only the light itself, present and specific. Attending.

I looked at it. I had been in the deep sea enough times to understand that light down here was not incidental. Light in the hadal zone was produced by organisms for specific purposes: to attract, to warn, to communicate, to see. Every deep-sea bioluminescent display was a signal of some kind, evolved over millions of years in conditions where the alternative to signalling was invisibility. There was no decorative bioluminescence. There was no accidental bioluminescence. Everything that made light down here made it on purpose.

This light was made on purpose. That purpose was to be seen by us.

Something was looking at us.

I do not know how long we sat there. Time had gone strange in the sphere — the specific temporal strangeness of situations in which your nervous system is overwhelmed and your processing cannot keep up with your experience. It might have been a minute. It might have been longer. The instruments would tell me later. While it was happening, I had no access to duration.

What I had access to was the light.

I will try to describe it accurately and I will fail, because accurate description requires a vocabulary for this and the vocabulary does not exist. What I can say is that the light was — both things at once, with no resolution between them. It was frightening. It was the most frightening thing I had encountered in almost four decades of being alive. And it was beautiful. Not beautiful in spite of the fear, not beautiful in a way that mitigated the fear, but beautiful in the same register and at the same intensity, simultaneously, as though the two responses were aspects of the same thing and could not be separated from each other any more than a temperature could be separated from what was producing it.

I was afraid. I was also watching something that no human being had ever watched before, in conditions that no human being had ever occupied before, and whatever was producing that light had come here and had outlined our vehicle and had stopped at our viewport because it knew, in some way I was not able to characterise, that the viewport was where we were.

It knew we were inside.

It was looking at us the way we look at things we want to understand.

* * *

Reyes said: "Mara."

I said: "I know."

"I'm logging this."

"I know."

He was logging it. I could see on the instrument panel that the camera systems were running, the passive acoustic array was recording the active channel alongside the environmental data, the timestamped log was filling with sensor readings. He was doing what he did: making the record. Making sure that whatever happened next, there was data.

The light did not move. It stayed at the viewport, attending. The DSV was still at forty percent power to the external lights. Nothing else had changed.

I thought about sending the sequence again. I thought about it for a long time — about what sending it again would mean, whether it would be understood as confirmation or as repetition, whether there was a meaningful distinction. I thought about Yuna's notebook: this is a language. I thought about what you said in a language when someone looked at you through a window for the first time.

I thought: I don't know enough yet.

I thought: I know enough to know that I don't know enough.

And then the light moved again — not away, not departing, but expanding slightly, spreading from the concentrated point at the viewport outward along the hull once more, a slow and deliberate redistribution, and in the expansion there was something that I cannot describe as anything other than a gesture. Not a human gesture. Not anything I had a reference for. But a movement with intent behind it, a movement that meant something even though I could not have said what, the way certain pieces of music mean something even when you cannot articulate what.

Then it was gone. Not faded — gone, the way a light goes when the source stops rather than when the light disperses. One moment present, the next absent.

The external lights came back up to full power immediately. The acoustic display returned to flat baseline. The instruments showed normal readings across every system. The structure below us was still.

The sphere was very quiet. The three of us in it were very quiet.

After a while, Stig said: "Do you want me to hold position?"

I looked at Reyes. He looked back at me.

He said: "Hold position."

We held position. The acoustic display stayed flat. The lights outside stayed steady. The Norwegian Sea went about whatever it went about in the dark at 3,100 metres, and the structure below us was still, and there was nothing to see or hear or record.

But I could still feel the place on my chest where the sequence had arrived through the hull, and I could still see the cold specific blue-green of the light against the glass, and I knew — not from analysis, not from inference, but from the simple fact of having been present — that what had just happened was not a phenomenon. It was an encounter.

Something had come to us. Something had looked at us. Something had gone away again.

And I did not know, sitting in that sphere at 3,100 metres while Reyes filled the log with clipped factual entries that were entirely inadequate for what they were describing, whether what had looked at us had found what it was looking for.

FIFTEEN

Ascent

We held position for eleven more minutes. I know the exact duration because Reyes logged it — Holding position post-contact event, 11 minutes, no further acoustic or visual activity detected — and I was watching the log update on the instrument panel in the same way I watched the acoustic display: not because I expected it to change, but because watching it gave my eyes somewhere to be that was not the viewport and not Reyes and not my own hands.

At the end of eleven minutes he said, quietly, "Stig. Take us up."

I did not argue. I had argued about the documentation survey and won an hour, and an hour had been the right call, and I had nothing equivalent to offer now. What I would have been arguing for was more time in the place where the thing had happened, and more time there was not a scientific position. It was something else, and I wasn't going to name it.

"Ascending," Stig said.

The thrusters shifted pitch. The depth display began to count upward. Below us, the structure receded into the dark.

* * *

The ascent took two hours and eight minutes by the log. I read this later; during the ascent I had no reliable sense of time passing. What I had was the depth display, which I watched, and the acoustic monitoring display, which showed the flat line returning to the ambient acoustic profile of the Norwegian Sea in the reverse order of its disappearance — the silence held until we passed 2,800 metres, and then the world came back: the geological background, the faint distant shipping, the low reliable sound of a living ocean.

I had not understood, until it returned, how much the silence had been doing to me.

The three of us did not talk during the ascent. This was not an agreement — we did not decide to be silent, did not look at each other and confirm the decision. We simply were. Stig ran the ascent with his usual competent attention, adjusting the rate at the correct depth intervals, checking the systems at the intervals the operational protocol required, making his log entries. Reyes made his own entries. I watched the displays.

I thought about the bioluminescence.

I had been thinking about it continuously since the light went out, in the way you thought about something that your processing could not complete — circling it, approaching it from different angles, reaching the same point of incompletion each time. Not the fact of it, which was established. Not even the meaning of it, which I was not yet equipped to assess. I was thinking about the specific experience of it: the way the fear and the beauty had been the same thing, inseparable, each intensifying the other rather than cancelling it, a response I had never had before to anything in my professional or personal life and for which I had no framework.

I was a scientist. I had a scientist's relationship with unknown things: curiosity, methodology, the reliable assumption that unknown things became known things if you asked the right questions in the right order. This had served me for thirty-eight years. It was not, at this moment, serving me, because the experience I was processing did not fit in the category of unknown things that became known things. It fit in a different category, one I had not previously needed, and I was doing the uncomfortable work of building that category in real time while ascending through two kilometres of dark Norwegian Sea water in a titanium sphere.

What I was building was something like: things that change you before you understand them.

The depth display read 1,900 metres. I watched it.

* * *

At 1,600 metres, Reyes said: "The log."

I looked at the instrument panel. His entries were visible on the shared display — I had been reading them in fragments throughout the ascent, the way you read something peripheral when your main attention is elsewhere. His entries for the post-encounter period read:

14.00: Active emitter deployed. Inverted calibration sequence transmitted. Standard operational protocol for acoustic survey.

14.01: Emitter silent. Passive array: baseline.

14.02: External lights reduced to approximately 40% output. No power system fault. Duration: ongoing at time of entry.

14.03: Passive acoustic detection. Low-frequency sequence, 83-second duration, consistent with previously documented pattern. Source: direct below, estimated 10m. Transmission received through hull as vibrational input.

14.05: Active emitter deployed. Inverted calibration sequence transmitted. Second transmission.

14.07: Bioluminescent event. External. Duration approximately 4 minutes. Location: hull perimeter and forward viewport. No instrument anomalies recorded. Cause: unknown.

14.11: External lights returned to full output. Passive array: baseline. All systems nominal.

I read this twice. *Cause: unknown* was doing an amount of work in that entry that the phrase was not designed for. *Standard operational protocol for acoustic survey* was doing the same work in the entries above it. Everything in the log was technically accurate. Nothing in the log was adequate.

"You're going to leave it as *unknown*," I said.

He looked at me. "I'm going to leave it as *unknown* until I know what it was."

"You know what it was."

"I know what it might have been. That's not the same thing."

I thought about this. He was right, technically. What we had was an encounter with a phenomenon that was consistent with intelligence — consistent with a great many things that intelligence would explain and that nothing else explained as well — but consistency was not proof. I had spent twelve years in an institution that did not accept consistency as proof.

"What are you going to report?" I said.

"The truth."

I looked at the log entries. At *cause: unknown*. At *standard operational protocol for acoustic survey*.

"Which truth?" I said.

He didn't answer. He looked at the depth display for a moment, then back at the log. He did not answer for the remaining sixteen hundred metres of ascent, and I did not ask again, and we rose through the mesopelagic and into the epipelagic and the light came back and the surface appeared above us as the hammered pewter it had been when we'd left it, and Stig said, "Surfacing," and we broke through.

* * *

The Norwegian Sea was grey and flat and cold and it was the most ordinary thing I had ever seen in my life. I sat in the pressure sphere while Stig ran the post-dive checks and the crane hook found the lifting point and the Lofoten's deck crew brought us up, and I looked out the viewport at the sky — pale, overcast, the specific Norwegian grey that meant weather coming — and I thought: this is the same sky it was this morning. The same ocean. The same vessel.

Everything above the surface was exactly as we had left it.

The hatch opened and cold air came in, the real cold of the Norwegian Sea in late August, and I climbed out and stood on the Lofoten's aft deck and looked at the water and thought about what was three kilometres below it.

Yuna was waiting at the edge of the work area. She had her notebook. She looked at my face and said nothing, which was characteristic — she read what my face was doing and concluded, correctly, that whatever I had to say I was not ready to say yet.

Reyes was already talking to the navigator. Operational debrief, post-dive systems check, the logistical machinery of having been somewhere and come back. He had his professional face on — not closed, not evasive, simply operational, the face of a man managing necessary tasks. I watched him from across the deck and thought about which truth he was deciding between.

I went to the rail and looked at the water.

It was the same water it had always been. It was not the same water it had always been. Both of these things were true and I was not going to resolve them standing at the Lofoten's rail in late August with weather coming in from the west.

After a while Yuna came and stood beside me. She did not say anything. This was the most useful thing she could have done.

The sea moved.

* * *

In the Lofoten's operations log — the official record, the one that would be filed with the institute and with the maritime authority and with whatever government bodies Reyes's institutional channels required — the second dive was described as a follow-up acoustic survey with no significant findings. The note in the log read: Active sonar survey conducted. Standard calibration protocols observed. No anomalous returns detected. All systems nominal.

Reyes had written this entry and I had read it before he filed it and I had not said anything, because the entry was written in the official log and the official log was not the place for what we had found, and both of us knew that and had not needed to discuss it.

In my own journal — locked, in my cabin, handwritten — I wrote two pages. I wrote everything: the dimming lights, the sequence through the hull, the emitter, the bioluminescence, the tracing of our outline, the light at the viewport. I wrote it in order, as precisely as I could, in the specific way I had been trained to record observations that could not yet be classified. I wrote: this was an encounter. I wrote: something looked at us.

I did not write what I thought it meant, because I did not yet know what I thought it meant. I knew what the data was. I knew what it felt like. I knew that the gap between those two things was larger than any gap I had encountered in twelve years of scientific work, and that crossing it was going to require more than I currently had.

I locked the journal. I turned off the cabin light. Outside, the weather Reyes had predicted was coming in — I could hear the change in the sea, the particular register of a rising wind, the Lofoten beginning to move with more purpose at her moorings.

I thought about the porthole light. About the person at the desk. About the structure and its careful offset rows and the specific quality of its surfaces. About the bioluminescence moving along our hull as though reading us.

I thought: it was studying us. The same way we were studying it.

I thought: it has been studying us for longer.

I fell asleep before I had finished the thought, which was, I understood when I woke in the early morning, probably the kindest thing my body had done for me in months.

Three kilometres below, in the dark at the floor of the Norwegian Sea, in the structure that extended two hundred metres in every direction from the point where a drilling rig had been placed with careful precision and its hatches sealed and its crew kept alive for eighty-five days, something moved through the forms in their offset rows. Unhurried. It did not have urgency in the way that surface creatures had urgency, because urgency was a response to scarcity of time and time was not scarce here.

But it was purposeful.

The surface-beings had come back. One of them had answered the signal. One of them had sent the inverted sequence, which was the correct response, which was the response that the original sequence had been designed, four hundred million years ago, to elicit. One of them had sat in her small bright sphere at the edge of the hadal zone and looked at the light and not looked away.

A decision had been made.

SIXTEEN

The Report

The call was at 06.00 the following morning, Reyes in the Lofoten's small communications room with the door locked and the encrypted channel open and a cup of coffee he didn't drink. His CO was Vice Admiral Chen, who had worked with him twice before and understood, without requiring explanation, that when Reyes asked for a secure line at six in the morning it was not because he had run out of things to do.

Chen had the quality that Reyes valued in commanding officers: he listened first and questioned second, in that order, and the questions he asked were the ones that mattered rather than the ones that were convenient. He did not have Harlow's gift for institutional brevity; he had something different, which was the patience of a man who had learned early in his career that the most important information in any report was what the reporting officer was most reluctant to include.

Reyes had spent the previous evening deciding what he was most reluctant to include. The decision had taken three hours and the better part of a bottle of Norwegian mineral water and a walk around the Lofoten's deck in the rain. He had reached a conclusion that he was not satisfied with and was going to act on anyway, which was not a position he found comfortable but was one he had occupied before.

"Reyes," Chen said. "Go."

He went.

* * *

He began with the rig. He described the Aurora Seven's condition in precise operational terms: structural integrity intact, all external systems functional, hatches sealed from outside with an organic substance of unknown composition and origin, chemical sensor readings on file and available for laboratory analysis. Position 3.2 kilometres from last logged coordinates. No evidence of implosion or catastrophic structural failure. No evidence of uncontrolled descent.

"Conclusion on the structural evidence?" Chen said.

"The rig was moved," Reyes said. "Placed at the current location deliberately. The precision of the positioning and the condition of the structure are not consistent with any failure mode I'm aware of."

A pause. "Moved by what?"

"Unknown at this time."

"Moved how?"

"Unknown. No external mechanical damage consistent with a towing or lifting operation. No visible attachment points or contact marks on the hull."

Another pause. Chen said: "All right. The crew."

"One individual confirmed present inside the structure. Visual confirmation through porthole at 3,100 metres. Seated position, alert posture, no apparent distress or incapacitation. Twenty-three additional crew presumed aboard based on manifest; not directly observed during the survey."

"Alert," Chen said.

"Alert."

"At three thousand metres."

"Yes."

"For eighty-five days."

"Eighty-five days as of the observation date, yes."

The silence on the line had a texture to it. Reyes had been in enough secure communications to distinguish between the silence of a man who was processing and the silence of a man who was deciding how to respond, and what he heard now was closer to the first.

Chen said: "You believe they're alive."

"Yes."

"Physically unharmed."

"The individual I observed showed no visible signs of physical distress. I was unable to communicate with them — the acoustic system was not able to penetrate the hull to their location, or they chose not to respond. I cannot confirm health status beyond visual observation."

"What's keeping them alive? Oxygen, water, food?"

"Unknown. The rig's internal systems may still be operational. We did not attempt to breach the hull or the hatch seals during this survey."

"Why not?"

This was the question Reyes had expected and had prepared an answer for. "Operational risk assessment. The hatch seals are of unknown composition and structural purpose. Breaching them without understanding their function posed an unacceptable risk to the crew's current condition and to the structural integrity of our own vehicle."

"And the real reason?" Chen said.

Reyes looked at the locked door of the communications room. He said: "Because I didn't know what had put the seals there, and I didn't think disturbing them was within the authority of a maritime safety audit."

A long pause. "Fair enough," Chen said. "Go on."

* * *

He described the structure. He was careful here — more careful than he had been with the rig, because the rig had a reference frame and the structure did not. He described the anomalous seafloor formations in terms of their observable properties: the distribution, the spacing, the surface characteristics, the extent. He did not use the words built or grown or biological, though each of them was available and accurate. He said: formations of unknown origin, inconsistent with standard geological process, requiring further analysis for classification. He said: estimated extent greater than two hundred metres radius. He said: chemical sensor readings on file.

Chen said: "Your assessment of origin?"

"Unknown."

"Geological?"

"Inconsistent with known geological processes in this region."

"Biological?"

"The surface characteristics of the formations are more consistent with biogenic origin than geological, but I want laboratory analysis of the sensor data before I commit to that classification."

"What does biogenic origin mean in this context?"

"It means produced by living organisms. It does not specify what kind."

Chen was quiet for a moment. Then: "Reyes. How large are we talking? In terms of what kind of organism could produce structures on this scale."

"I would rather not speculate until I have the laboratory data."

"That's not an answer."

"No," Reyes said. "It isn't."

Another silence. Chen said: "What are you not telling me?"

Reyes had known this was coming. He had known it because Chen asked it every time, on every operation, in every debrief where the reporting officer had left a gap. It was his most reliable technique and Reyes respected it and had been sitting with the answer to it for three hours.

He said: "I have observations from the site that I am not yet able to characterise accurately enough to report. I'm withholding them until I can provide a complete and accurate account. I will have a supplementary report for you within seventy-two hours."

The pause this time was the longest yet. "You know what that sounds like," Chen said.

"Yes."

"It sounds like a man who found something he doesn't know how to put in a report."

"Yes," Reyes said.

"Is what you found a threat to national security?"

Reyes thought about this with the specific care it deserved. "I don't believe so. Not in any immediate or direct sense."

"Is it a threat to the crew of the Aurora Seven?"

"No. The evidence is consistent with the crew being maintained in good condition."

"Is whatever is down there aware that you were there?"

The question arrived precisely, which was characteristic of Chen, and Reyes sat with it for a moment before answering.

"Yes," he said. "I believe so."

"And it didn't act against you."

"No."

"All right," Chen said. "Seventy-two hours. I want the supplementary report personally and through the encrypted channel only. Nothing goes into the standard reporting chain until I've seen it." A pause. "What do you recommend in the interim?"

"Nothing," Reyes said. "Yet."

* * *

He had expected Chen to push back on this. Chen did not push back. He said: "Understood. One more thing."

"Go ahead."

"NordDepth filed an application with the Norwegian Offshore Directorate three days ago for operational resumption at the Aurora Seven site. New rig, same location. The application is working through the regulatory channels, but given the circumstances, there's no obvious legal basis to deny it. Current estimate for deployment: three weeks."

Reyes looked at his untouched coffee. "Moen is deploying another rig."

"The application is his company's, yes. Whether he believes the site is safe or whether he's demonstrating that he believes it, I can't tell you. His lawyers have been active."

"He knows the site isn't safe."

"Does he?"

"I told him the frequency readings were consistent across multiple independent operations. He told me his engineering team had confirmed the same thing." Reyes paused. "He's not a stupid man."

"No," Chen said. "But he's in a difficult position legally and commercially, and the path of least resistance is to proceed as though what happened to the Aurora Seven was an anomaly. Three weeks is not much time."

"No," Reyes said. "It isn't."

He thought about the structure extending two hundred metres in every direction from the point where the Aurora Seven had been placed. He thought about the hatch seals and the person at the desk and the bioluminescence tracing the outline of their vehicle, and he thought about a new rig arriving at that site in three weeks with a crew who knew nothing about what was there.

"I'll have the supplementary report to you in seventy-two hours," he said.

"Good," Chen said. "Reyes."

"Sir."

"Whatever you found. I need you to understand that the window for handling this quietly is not infinite."

"I understand."

"Seventy-two hours."

The call ended.

* * *

Reyes sat in the communications room for a while after the call. The coffee was cold. Outside, the Lofoten was making the specific sounds of a vessel preparing to get underway — he could hear the engine room from here, the change in the generators' pitch that preceded departure, the occasional clatter of deck activity.

He thought about the supplementary report.

He had told Chen he would provide one in seventy-two hours, and he would. He had told Chen he was withholding observations that he couldn't yet characterise accurately enough to report, and this was true. What he had not told Chen — what he had not told anyone — was the specific nature of the observations he was withholding or why characterising them accurately was proving difficult.

The difficulty was not technical. He had the camera footage, the acoustic recordings, the instrument logs. The data was complete and clear. The difficulty was that accurately characterising the bioluminescent event, and Mara's signal exchange, and the sequence arriving through the hull, required him to choose a classification for what had produced them, and the available classifications were two: natural phenomenon of unknown type, or something else entirely.

He was not ready to put something else entirely in a report to a Vice Admiral.

Not yet. Not without more information. Not without knowing whether what had looked at them through the viewport of the DSV was something that could be reported accurately or something that would, once reported, immediately become the property of processes that neither he nor Mara could influence or control.

He thought about Mara. He thought about what she had said on the ascent — which truth — and about the fact that he hadn't answered her, and about the fact that she had known he hadn't answered because he didn't have the answer yet, not because he was evading the question.

He thought: she is going to ask me again.

He thought: I will need to have a better answer by then.

He picked up the cold coffee, looked at it, and put it down again. He unlocked the communications room door and went out onto the deck into the rain, which was still coming down with the flat persistence of Norwegian late-summer rain, the kind that was not violent but was comprehensive, the kind that covered everything.

Across the deck, at the stern rail, Mara was standing with her back to him looking at the water. She was wearing a yellow offshore jacket that was too large for her and had her hands in the front pocket. She did not turn around.

He stood there for a moment. Then he went back inside to start the supplementary report.

Three weeks. He wrote that down first, at the top of the first page, as a reminder to himself of the operative constraint. Everything else would be shaped by that number. What he could afford to take time over, and what he couldn't. What could wait for laboratory confirmation, and what couldn't. What he was going to tell Chen, and what he was going to need to tell Mara first.

He wrote: Aurora Seven site. New operational deployment. Three weeks.

He looked at it. Then he started writing.

SEVENTEEN

The Watcher

[What follows is a translation. All translations are approximations. This one more than most.]

There is no now, exactly.

There is the deep ridge where the water is cold enough to hold memory, and in that memory there is the signal — the first signal, the one that came from above four years ago in the surface-species' frequency, carrying the old ratio that the deep had not heard from a surface creature in longer than this particular body had been individual. There is that signal and there is this moment and the distance between them is not time in the way that surface creatures experienced time, not a line but a texture, a temperature, the way the water held both events without distinguishing between them.

Sable — which was not a name but was the approximation that would be used by those who needed names for things — attended.

Attending was not the right word either. There was no single place to attend from. Sable's awareness was distributed across the body's full extent: the chemoreceptors along the outer surface reading the water's information, the pressure-sensitive arrays along the flanks processing the acoustic environment, the electromagnetic organs — located in no single region, emerging from no single cell cluster — registering the ridge's low background field and the subtle variations in it that carried the community's traffic. To say Sable attended was to say a forest attended. Technically true in aggregate. Misleading about the mechanism.

But the surface-creatures' languages had no word for what Sable was doing, so: attending.

* * *

The signal had come in the old ratio. Two parts to one. The ratio that the deep had used for communication before there were fish in the shallows, before there were shallows, before the ocean had its current chemistry. The ratio that encoded presence: *I am here and I am structured and my structure is legible.*

No surface creature had sent this ratio in 200,000 years. Not deliberately.

The one that had come before — before the long watch, before the decision to wait — had not been a creature with language as the deep understood language. It had been a creature with signal, which was a different thing. Signal was the beginning. Language was what signal became across sufficient time and sufficient pressure to refine it.

This creature — this surface-being, this Mara-shape pressing her small warm hand against the viewport glass — had sent the ratio in the old frequency. Not knowing what it was. The instruments said not-knowing: the response had come after a pause that was consistent with recognition rather than composition, and the inversion she had sent was a mirror, not a translation. She had received a pattern and sent back its reflection.

But.

She had done it correctly.

She had sat with the uncertainty rather than resolving it.

She had looked at the light and not looked away.

These three things together constituted something. Sable had no human word for the category. The closest approximation would be: *a mind that could be spoken to.*

* * *

The community processed the encounter continuously in the days that followed, the way it processed everything continuously — not in sequence, not in sessions, but as a persistent thread of distributed attention that ran through all members within contact range. What Sable had observed was in the community now, available to any member who attended to that frequency. What the community thought about it was also available, which was how thinking worked here: not inside a single location but across the network, positions emerging and dissolving as the conversation moved through.

The dominant position, which was the largest faction's position, which was the Watchers' position:

The surface-species is not ready. Has not been ready. Will not be ready within any interval we have observed surface-species become ready. The silence has held for 200,000 years. What happened with the signal was a proximity event, not an invitation. The correct response is continued observation.

This position had the weight of duration behind it. Two hundred thousand years was a short time by Sable's measure — Sable had individual memories going back further than that — but it was 200,000 years of the same conclusion, reinforced each time new surface-species data was added to the community record. The surface-species were remarkable. They were also, in the judgment of the Watchers, fragile in a specific way: not physically fragile, not intellectually fragile, but structurally fragile in the way that a thing was fragile when its growth was not yet complete and contact with something much older would deform rather than develop it.

The Watchers were not wrong, Sable acknowledged. Sable had examined their position many times across many years and had found it internally consistent and its premises well-supported. The surface-species were young. Their civilisation was approximately five thousand years old, which was not even a rounding error against the deep's history. Their technology was extraordinary for its age but had produced, in the last two hundred of those five thousand years, consequences that threatened the chemistry of the ocean to a depth that was new in the deep's memory of surface-species behaviour.

The Watchers were not wrong about the surface-species.

They were wrong about the interval.

* * *

Three things had changed. The community had processed this many times; Sable had processed it many times. Processing did not always change positions. Sometimes it only clarified them.

The structures.

The surface-species' extraction machines had been advancing into deep water for forty of their years, and the rate was increasing, and the machines had no awareness of what they were destroying. This was not hostility. Hostility Sable could work with, because hostility was a relationship and relationships could be altered. This was indifference, which was harder, because indifference required the indifferent party to first be made aware that there was something to be indifferent to.

The chemistry.

The ocean's thermal and chemical profile had been shifting across Sable's full lifespan in ways that were within the range of historical variation but were moving in a direction that the community's models, extended forward across several centuries, produced results that had not been seen in the deep's recorded memory. The community was not alarmed in the way surface-species experienced alarm — there was no single body to flood with adrenaline, no localised fear response. But the community was attentive in a new way, a way that was adjacent to what surface-species called concern.

The signal.

Four years ago, a research vessel had emitted the old ratio from above. Not knowing what it was. The ratio had propagated down through 4,200 metres of water and arrived at the ridge with the specific character of a greeting under the oldest protocol — the protocol the deep had established when the deep still half-believed it might one day speak with something on the surface. The protocol that had not been triggered in the deep's entire experience of surface life, because no surface creature had ever, before this, produced a signal with the old ratio's structure.

Sable had received it. Sable had replied.

And then the surface-being had come back. Into the deep. Into the zone of silence. Had looked at the structure and had not destroyed it and had not fled. Had looked at the sealed rig and at the person inside and had not tried to break the seals but had placed a hand on the glass. Had sent the inverted sequence. Had held position for eleven minutes after the light departed, neither advancing nor retreating, before ascending.

Had sat with the uncertainty.

* * *

Sable brought the case to the Bridge.

The Bridge was not a place. It was a frequency, a pattern of attention, a current in the community's distributed processing that was characterised by the position it held: *contact is necessary, not because the surface-species is ready, but because the alternative to contact is a collision that neither species can survive intact.*

The Bridge had been a minority position for as long as Sable could remember. But it was a position that the three changes had strengthened, incrementally, across the forty years in which the machines had come deeper and the chemistry had shifted and the ocean's future had become a variable rather than a constant.

Sable presented the surface-being.

She sent the inverted sequence. The correct response. Without instruction.

She looked at the light and did not flinch. She remained in proximity to the unknown for eleven of her time-units before ascending.

She is not, by the community's consensus measures, ready. But she is of the type that can become ready. This is rare. This is the condition we have been watching for.

The Bridge attended.

The new machine arrives in three of their weeks. If we do not speak before it arrives, we cannot speak after. The machine will damage the structure again. The Watchers will respond. The collision course will be established without our participation in its direction.

If we speak now, through this one, through the surface-being who answered — we may be able to place ourselves in the interval between the collision and its consequences. We may be able to speak before the Watchers act. We may not. But the window exists now and will not exist again.

The community processed this. The Bridge processed it within itself, which was a smaller processing, a subset of the whole.

There were objections. There were always objections; the Bridge had not been a majority position for a reason.

The surface-being cannot speak our language. She has a translation of a translation of a fraction. This is not communication. This is gesture.

Gesture is how language begins.

We have no evidence she speaks for anyone other than herself.

This is true. But she answered correctly without authorisation. She answered as herself. The community's record shows that surface-species who act from authorisation do not hear what they are told; surface-species who act from themselves sometimes do.

This had weight. The community felt it. The surface-being's response had been unsanctioned, which by the community's record of surface-species behaviour made it more reliable rather than less. She had acted without institutional cover. She had acted as a single mind deciding in the moment what to do next. The community's long watch had shown that surface-species acting from institutional authority tended to perform rather than to listen, while surface-species acting from themselves sometimes produced the unexpected — including, occasionally, the ability to hear what was being said.

This was the type.

* * *

The argument took time. Time in the deep sense — not hours or days, which were surface-species measurements and had no direct translation, but the span of the community's attention across the question. The Watchers were not part of this processing. They would be informed of the outcome.

Sable was aware, throughout, of the rig on the seafloor. Of the twenty-four surface-beings inside it, in their sealed environment, who had been in the deep's care for what their biology experienced as a very long time. They were being sustained. The community had seen to that, had seen to it with the same attention that the deep gave to any fragile thing that entered its territory. They were not harmed. Some of them had begun, in the way that long exposure to the deep sometimes produced in surface creatures, to hear. Very faintly. Very incompletely. But the frequency was getting through.

They could not be kept indefinitely. Their biology was not built for the deep. The surface-being who had come down in her small bright sphere had confirmed that the surface-species knew the sealed ones were there — had seen one of them, had pressed her hand to the glass. The surface-species would come back for them. When they came back, the encounter would be determined by whoever arrived first and whatever their intentions were.

This was the argument's urgency: not the new machine alone, but the fact that the next contact was coming regardless of the deep's preference. The question was whether the deep participated in shaping it.

The Bridge voted.

It was not a vote in the surface-species sense — a counted binary, one side or the other. It was a resonance, a frequency either present or absent across the network of members who held the Bridge position. The resonance built slowly, not unanimously, with pockets of resistance and uncertainty that remained after the dominant direction was clear.

The dominant direction was clear.

We will speak. Through the one who answered. Before the machine arrives.

We will speak now.

In the structure above the ridge, in the space that the surface-species' instruments had logged as geological formations and unusual rock configurations and anomalous sonar returns, something shifted.

It was not an action in the surface-species sense. It was a change of state — the way a key change in music was a change of state, everything altered without anything stopping, the same notes in a different relationship to each other. The community had been watching. Now it was preparing.

The surface-being who answered was on the vessel above. She did not sleep. She stood at a rail in the dark and looked at the water.

She had looked at the light and not looked away.

That was enough.

It would have to be enough.

ACT THREE

The Signal

EIGHTEEN

The Approach

I had gone to bed. I had not slept.

This had been the pattern for several weeks, the not-sleeping: my body doing its best impression of rest while my mind ran its data on a loop that had no natural stopping point. The bioluminescence. The sequence through the hull. Reyes's log entries. Chen's three weeks. The person at the desk in the porthole light. I would arrive at one of these things and it would lead to another and another and eventually back to the start, and the loop would run again, and at some point the sky would lighten and I would get up.

That night the loop ran until approximately 02.40, at which point I gave up, put on my clothes and my offshore jacket and went out to the stern deck.

The rain had stopped. The Norwegian Sea was flat, which it rarely was, a flat that was not calm so much as suspended — the water holding itself in a temporary stillness the way a breath was held before something was said. The sky was overcast, no stars, the dark between the vessel's lights absolute. To the east, very faintly, the suggestion of the ridge topography in the sonar display visible through the data deck window. To the north and south and west: nothing. Open water.

I stood at the rail and looked at it and thought about nothing specific, which was as close to not-thinking as I could get.

At 03.04, the water near the stern began to glow.

* * *

Not diffusely. Not the way bioluminescence appeared when you disturbed plankton-rich water, the general shimmer of a million small organisms responding to movement. In a pattern.

I recognised it before I fully understood that I was recognising it. The same way you recognised music you had heard before you consciously identified the piece — the pattern arrived in me as familiarity before it arrived as analysis. Six pulses at the two-to-one interval. Brief pause. Six pulses.

On the surface of the Norwegian Sea. At 3am. In bioluminescence visible from the stern deck of the Lofoten.

I did not move for a moment. I was aware, with the specific clarity that arrived sometimes in the middle of the night when all the social and institutional scaffolding of daylight thinking was absent, that this was the moment the loop had been preparing me for without my knowing it. The data deck. The archive. The 2019 calibration. The months of running the same sequence through every filter I had. All of it had been preparation for this specific instant on this specific deck and I had not known it was preparation because preparation looked exactly like obsession from the inside.

Something was close. Not in the submersible, not recorded on instruments. Present, at the surface, in water I could have reached by leaning over the rail.

I went to get my equipment.

* * *

The data deck was empty. Magnus had the overnight watch on the bridge; the rest of the crew was asleep. I pulled the portable hydrophone unit from the equipment locker — a small handheld system, battery-powered, designed for surface acoustic monitoring, not the deep-water capability of the towed array but sufficient for close-range detection — and brought it back to the stern deck with the tablet that served as its display.

The bioluminescence was still there. It had moved while I was below — not drifted, moved, the same purposeful quality I had seen in the deep, the pattern shifting position in a way that tracking the hull suggested: the pulses traced a slow arc along the port side of the Lofoten's waterline and back, maintaining a consistent distance of approximately three metres from the hull. Not touching. Attending.

I set up the hydrophone at the stern rail and lowered the sensor element into the water.

Immediately the tablet display showed signal. Low-frequency, in the correct range, strong — considerably stronger than anything I'd detected from the surface in previous surveys. The sequence was present and active and whatever was producing it was not three kilometres below me. It was here.

I looked at the display for a moment. Then I looked at the water, where the bioluminescence pulsed in the same rhythm as the signal on the display, the light and the acoustic output synchronised, two channels carrying the same information.

The acoustic emitter on the portable unit was limited — nothing like the DSV's system, not designed for directional transmission, but capable of producing a pulse in the correct frequency range. I had the calibration sequence parameters saved on the tablet from the deep dive. I called them up.

I looked at the water one more time. The light pulsed. The display pulsed. Six and six and six, the old ratio, patient and exact.

I transmitted.

* * *

The response was immediate. Not eleven seconds — immediate, within two seconds of my transmission completing, as though whatever was below had been waiting not for the right moment but for the transmission to finish before beginning its reply.

And the reply was different.

Not the original sequence returned, not the mirror I had received in the deep. This was longer. Considerably longer. The tablet display showed signal running for nearly four minutes — a continuous transmission, structured, internally complex in a way that the familiar six-pulse pattern was not. The bioluminescence changed with it: the steady pulsing shifted into something more varied, the light moving in shapes that I couldn't resolve into specifics from where I stood but that were clearly not random, clearly not the simple on-off of the original sequence.

I recorded all of it. I had the hydrophone input logging to the tablet's storage, the video from the deck camera running, my own voice on the audio capture noting timestamps and observations. I was aware, even while doing all of this, of something that I can only describe as the difference between a subject and a conversation — I had been studying a subject for months, and now the subject had turned and was addressing me, and the two activities were not the same thing at all and required different equipment than I had available.

When the transmission ended, I stood at the rail for a moment.

Then I went to wake Yuna.

* * *

She was awake when I knocked. I heard her moving before I'd finished the second knock, which was characteristic — Yuna's sleep had the quality of a system in standby rather than a system fully off.

I said: "Come to the stern deck. Bring everything."

She said: "How long do I have?"

"I don't know. It's still there."

Three minutes later she was on the stern deck with her recording equipment, her notebook, and the expression she wore when something had moved beyond the theoretical into the actual — not excited, not alarmed, but wholly present, the full Yuna attention turned on like a lamp.

She looked at the water. The bioluminescence was still there, the pattern quieter now, no longer transmitting, holding position near the hull in steady low pulses. She looked at my tablet display, at the recording of the four-minute sequence. She sat down on the equipment case and put her headphones on and started listening.

I sat beside her and watched the water and waited.

The sky to the northeast was beginning to show the first grey suggestion of pre-dawn — a lightening that was not yet light, the dark becoming marginally less absolute. In a few hours the Norwegian summer morning would arrive and the watch would change and other people would be on deck, and this particular moment — just the two of us and the thing in the water and the four-minute recording — would be over.

Yuna listened for twenty minutes without speaking. She was making notes, not in the shorthand she used for routine documentation but in full sentences, which meant she was finding things fast enough to want to record them as they arrived. I watched the bioluminescence and did not interrupt her.

At the end of twenty minutes she took off the headphones and looked at the water.

"It's complex," she said. "The internal structure — there are recurring elements, but the arrangement isn't a simple repetition. It has the character of a sentence rather than a phrase."

"Can you decode it?"

"Not yet. Not with one pass. I need to understand the vocabulary before I can approach the syntax." She paused. "But there's something at the beginning. Before the complex structure starts. Can you play me the first forty seconds?"

I played her the first forty seconds.

She listened. She listened again. She picked up her notebook and wrote something and looked at it and wrote something else.

"Play me from the start to the first pause," she said. "Everything before the first internal gap."

I played it.

She was very still. The water moved. The bioluminescence pulsed once, twice, patient and unhurried.

"Yuna," I said.

She held up one finger. She was counting something. After a moment she lowered it.

"The opening sequence," she said. "The pattern before the first gap. Count the pulses."

I played it again and counted. "Ten."

"In groups of —"

I listened. "Two. Three. Five."

"Two, three, five," she said. "And if the sequence continued."

I saw it. My breath did something that was not quite catching, more a brief interruption, the way breathing interrupted itself when something arrived that the body recognised before the mind caught up. "Seven," I said. "Eleven. Thirteen."

"Prime numbers," Yuna said. "In sequence. From the beginning."

I looked at the water. The bioluminescence pulsed.

"That's not a coincidence," I said.

"No," she said. "It isn't. Prime numbers are the same in any mathematics. Any intelligence that uses mathematics will arrive at primes. They're a universal — a signal that says: this is structured, this is intentional, and the structure is one you will recognise." She looked at the display. "It's an introduction. Before everything else — before whatever the four minutes contain — it sent an introduction. Something we could not possibly mistake."

She said this last word quietly. I could not see her face clearly in the pre-dawn dark but I knew her well enough to know her expression: not awed, not frightened, but focused in the specific way she was focused when a theoretical framework she had been building for years suddenly had an object to attach to.

"It's talking to us," I said.

"Yes," she said. "And it knew we needed the introduction first." A pause. "It knows what we know. It knows what humans know about mathematics. It prepared this."

The sky was getting lighter. The bioluminescence was fading now — not disappearing, dimming, the way a lamp dimmed when the power source was reducing rather than cutting out. As though whatever was below was still there but withdrawing attention from the surface, the transmission complete, the introduction delivered, waiting for what came next.

Yuna was already working. She had the recording open, the analysis tools running, her headphones back on. She had a great deal to do and she knew it and she was doing it with the focused economy of someone who understood that what was in her hands was the most important material she would ever work with.

I sat beside her and watched the last of the bioluminescence fade into the ordinary grey of a Norwegian Sea dawn.

Whatever had come to the surface had chosen to come. It had not waited for us to return to the deep. It had come here, to our level, to the layer of water where we lived, and it had introduced itself in a language we could not mistake.

I thought about the new rig sitting in a Bergen harbour. I thought about Chen and his supplementary report. I thought about how little time we had.

I thought: the window is smaller than any of us understood.

I thought: something knows that. And it came up anyway.

NINETEEN

Language

Yuna worked the way she always worked when something was important: without stopping, without announcing what she was doing, without waiting to know where she was going before she started moving. She had been working since the pre-dawn session on the stern deck, through the morning and the afternoon and into the second night, with breaks for food that she ate at the workstation without tasting and sleep that lasted ninety minutes in the early afternoon before something in the data pulled her back.

The first session — the four-minute recording from the night before — had given her the introduction and something else: the beginning of a structure. Not the structure itself, which was still largely opaque, but its shadow. The way you could infer the presence of a building from the pattern of shadows it cast even before you could see the building directly.

What she had: a signal corpus that demonstrated compressed information encoding, confirmed by the frequency distribution analysis she'd run before departure. What she now had additionally: a four-minute transmission with internal recurrence — specific sub-sequences that appeared more than once, in different positions within the larger structure, in ways that were consistent with either vocabulary items or grammatical markers. She didn't know which yet. The distinction mattered enormously.

She built two hypotheses and ran them simultaneously, which was how she worked when she didn't yet know which was right.

Hypothesis one: the recurring sub-sequences were vocabulary — individual concepts, encoded as specific pressure-frequency-duration combinations, appearing wherever those concepts were relevant. This would be the simpler system, analogous to a word list rather than a grammar.

Hypothesis two: the recurring sub-sequences were structural — markers that indicated relationships between other elements, the way prepositions indicated spatial or logical relationships in human language. This would imply a more complex system with its own syntax.

By noon she had enough to suspect hypothesis two was at least partially correct. By mid-afternoon she was nearly certain. By the time the second night arrived and the bioluminescence returned to the stern deck, she had a working model of why.

* * *

The exchange sessions had a rhythm now. The thing below — Yuna had not named it, was carefully not naming it, because naming would collapse a set of possibilities she wasn't ready to collapse — would transmit. They would record. Mara would respond with the calibration sequence, which seemed to function as an acknowledgment, a signal that the transmission had been received. Then a pause, varying in length, after which the thing below would transmit again. Longer each time. More complex each time.

It was learning something from their responses, Yuna thought. Or testing something. The transmissions were not random variations — they were systematic in a way she was beginning to recognise. Each new transmission shared structural elements with the previous one but added something, extended something, introduced a new combination. As though it were presenting vocabulary in controlled increments, sequencing the new against the familiar the way a careful teacher introduced new material: here is something you have seen before, and here beside it is something you have not.

This was not coincidence. Whatever was below them had been watching the surface for longer than she could calibrate — longer than any human language had been in use, by an order of magnitude at minimum. It knew communication required shared ground. It was building the shared ground deliberately, one transmission at a time.

Yuna found this both extraordinary and, in a specific way she kept examining from different angles, deeply familiar. This was how language worked. How it had always worked. You started with the things you could both point at. You built toward the things you couldn't.

* * *

I watched Yuna work the way you watched someone do something you couldn't do but understood well enough to appreciate — with the specific combination of admiration and uselessness that came from being in the presence of a skill you would never have.

My contribution was the transmissions. I ran the hydrophone array and the emitter, I handled the acoustic recordings, I sent the calibration acknowledgments on Yuna's cue. This was not nothing — the technical operation of the exchange required constant attention — but it was not the work. The work was Yuna's. She was building something out of the transmissions that I could see taking shape in her notebooks and on her screens without yet being able to read it.

We had told Reyes at breakfast. He had listened to the recording from the first night without speaking, and then he had asked three questions — duration, frequency range, whether we had positively ruled out surface vessel activity as a source — and when we confirmed all three his expression had gone through something that I recognised as his processing face arriving at a conclusion he was not yet ready to name.

He had not interfered with the sessions. He had not tried to take over the emitter or supervise the exchange or contact Chen. He had eaten his meals, maintained the vessel's operational log, managed the crew's routine activities, and checked in with us every few hours in the specific Reyes way — arriving, looking at what we had, asking one precise question, leaving. He was giving us the space to work and I understood, without us discussing it, that this was a decision he had made and that it was costing him something to maintain it.

That evening, I saw him at the communications panel on the bridge. He was at the automated position reporting terminal — a system that sent the Lofoten's coordinates to the Norwegian Maritime Authority every four hours as standard safety protocol. I watched from the corridor as he navigated the menu, found the scheduled reports setting, and changed the transmission interval from four hours to forty-eight.

Not disabled. Not falsified. Extended. The system would still report. Just not as often.

He didn't look up. I went back to the stern deck.

* * *

The second night's sessions ran from 21.00 to 04.30 the following morning, with two breaks of twenty minutes each when the transmissions from below paused and nothing came. Yuna used the breaks to eat crackers and write up her notes in full sentences rather than shorthand, which she said helped her think.

I used them to stand at the rail and look at the water, which helped me do something I couldn't have named but that was necessary.

By midnight Yuna had mapped what she was calling the phonological layer — the basic units of the system, the individual pressure-frequency-duration combinations that appeared to function as the minimum meaningful elements. There were more of them than she had expected — not the dozens of phonemes in a human language but something closer to the hundreds of tones in a complex tonal system, where pitch, duration, and interval each carried independent information. The combinatorial space was large. The system was correspondingly rich.

"This is not a simple system," she said, not to me specifically, to the workstation, to the data. "This is not a communication system that evolved for basic signalling. This has the complexity profile of a language that has been in use for a very long time and has developed the kind of nuance that comes from very long use."

"How long?" I said.

She looked at me. "I have no way to calibrate that. Longer than any human language has been in use. By an order of magnitude, at minimum."

I thought about this. I thought about what that number would mean, applied to the complexity of a communication system. I thought about the fact that we did not yet have a name for what was below us, did not have a vocabulary for the category of thing we were in contact with, were working inside a gap in language that we would eventually have to fill but were not ready to fill yet. The implications of what Yuna had said were not something I was ready to introduce into our working session.

I said: "Keep going."

She kept going.

* * *

The breakthrough, when it arrived, arrived quietly. This was characteristic of Yuna's breakthroughs — they did not announce themselves. You recognised them only by the quality of her silence afterward, which was different from her working silence, more settled, the silence of someone who had stopped moving because they had arrived.

It was 02.17. She had been working with a specific sub-sequence that appeared in three of the evening's transmissions — the same combination of elements, always in the same position, always adjacent to what she had been tentatively calling the initiating element of a transmission. She had a hypothesis about it. She had been testing the hypothesis by constructing a small response — not the calibration acknowledgment but something more specific, a transmission that used the sub-sequence she was examining in a position that, if her hypothesis was correct, would constitute a statement rather than a reply.

She sent it. We waited.

The response came in under two seconds — faster than any previous response. A single, brief sequence. Four elements. Nothing she had seen before combined in quite that way.

Yuna listened to it twice. Then she wrote in her notebook in large letters and turned the notebook so I could read it:

PRESENCE confirmed.

I looked at her.

"The sub-sequence is a presence marker," she said. "It encodes the concept of being-here, of occupying this location, of this-exchange-is-happening. When I used it in my transmission, I was saying, in approximate terms: I am here. Its response confirmed that it received that meaning. The four-element sequence it sent back — I need more data to be certain, but my hypothesis is that it contains the same marker sent back at us. Here-also. Present-also."

"It said I am here too," I said.

"Approximately. Yes."

I looked at the water. The bioluminescence was there, the steady low pulses that had become, in the past two days, almost ordinary — something I looked for the way you looked for a light in a window you'd passed enough times to expect it.

"That's the first concept," I said.

"That's the first concept," she confirmed.

* * *

Recognition came ninety minutes later, in the session's seventh hour.

Yuna had been building on the presence marker — constructing responses that used it in different contexts, pairing it with other elements, watching how the transmissions from below varied in response. She was, she explained to me during a break, trying to understand the system's combinatorial rules: how elements combined, whether order mattered, whether repetition changed meaning. She was working inductively, the way you worked when you had no external reference, building a grammar from the inside out.

The concept of recognition emerged from a sequence that appeared every time Mara's calibration acknowledgment was sent. After two nights of exchanges, Yuna had noticed that this sequence appeared consistently in the position of a response to the acknowledgment, and that it was always the same, and that it was structurally distinct from everything else in the transmissions. She had a hypothesis: it was a marker for this-has-been-received-and-understood, the acknowledgment of an acknowledgment.

She tested it by sending the sequence herself, unprompted, in the middle of a pause between transmissions. The response was immediate — the same sequence returned, and then something new following it, an extension she hadn't seen before.

"It's recognising the recognition," she said. "I sent its acknowledgment marker back at it and it responded with — I need to think about this — I think it's an extension of the same concept. Recognised-by-me. An indication that the exchange is mutual, that both parties are aware of each other's awareness."

"Recognition," I said.

"In some form. The human concept maps imperfectly. But yes."

We sat with this for a moment, the second concept in hand, the water moving.

I thought: it knows we are here. It knows we know it is here. It knows we know it knows we are here. The mutual awareness was established not just as fact but as communicated fact, as something both parties had confirmed to each other. That confirmation was what made it real in the shared space between us.

I did not say this to Yuna. She was already moving toward the third concept and I didn't want to interrupt the momentum.

* * *

The third concept arrived at 04.11, nineteen minutes before the first grey light in the northeast.

It arrived differently from the first two — not through a hypothesis that Yuna tested and confirmed, but through a transmission from below that she spent forty minutes with before she said anything. The transmission was unlike anything they'd sent before: longer than the previous night's offerings, more internally varied, with a structure that Yuna said felt less like a statement and more like — she paused, searching — a form.

"A form," I said.

"An inflection. A change in the character of the whole transmission rather than a change in its content." She played me a section. "Hear that? The duration profile of the elements. The long-short-long pattern. In every human tonal language I've studied, and in the formal literature on communication theory, a distinctive durational pattern applied consistently across a transmission tends to function as a mood marker — it modifies everything else. Interrogative. Declarative. Imperative."

"It's asking something."

"I think so. I think that's what this is — not a new concept but a new mode. Everything in this transmission is inflected with something that functions like a question."

I looked at the display. At the transmission running on the screen, the waveform I had been staring at for two days resolving, under Yuna's analysis, into something with grammar. Something that bent toward us and waited.

"What is it asking?" I said.

Yuna was quiet for a moment. Outside, the pre-dawn grey was spreading. The bioluminescence had faded again, as it did each morning, the thing below withdrawing from the surface as the light returned as though it knew — and of course it knew, of course it had always known — where the boundary between its world and ours lay.

"I don't know yet," she said. "I don't have enough vocabulary to parse the content. I know the mode. I know it's asking. What it's asking" — she looked at the recording — "I'm going to need the day."

I nodded. I looked at the water, flat and grey now in the growing light, ordinary again, the surface restored to its surface character, concealing everything below it.

Somewhere three kilometres down, something was waiting for our answer.

We did not yet know the question.

Reyes found us at 05.00, when the watch changed and the crew began to stir. He came to the stern deck with two cups of coffee — one for me, one for Yuna, nothing for himself — and looked at the screens and the notebooks and the recording still playing on the display.

He said: "Three concepts."

"Two confirmed," Yuna said. "The third is a mode, not a concept. I know it's asking something. I don't know what."

He absorbed this the way he absorbed things: completely, without visible reaction. He handed over the coffees. He looked at the water.

After a moment he said: "I changed the position reporting interval last night. Forty-eight hours instead of four."

Yuna looked at him. I looked at the water.

"I know," I said.

A pause. "I'm not going to be able to hold that indefinitely."

"I know."

"But you need time to understand what it's asking before anything else happens."

"Yes."

He nodded. He looked at the water one more time, then back at Yuna's screens, at the waveform running in its loop, the question encoded in four minutes of pressure and frequency and duration that

Yuna was going to spend the day learning to read.

He said nothing else. He went back inside.

Yuna drank her coffee and opened her notebook to a fresh page.

Outside, the Norwegian Sea became morning.

TWENTY

Moen Moves

The footage arrived at 14.30 on a Friday, forwarded through a private channel by the intelligence contractor whose retainer Moen had authorised three weeks ago. He was in a budget meeting when it arrived. He excused himself, which was something he did rarely and which his CFO noted with the specific attention of a person accustomed to reading Moen's departures from routine.

He watched it in his office with the door closed.

The clip was forty-seven seconds. Shot from distance, at night, in low light — the footage quality was what you got from a surveillance vessel running dark at eight kilometres, and eight kilometres was a long way for a sensor array that was not designed for cetacean photography. What you could see: the stern section of a research vessel, identifiable by configuration as the Lofoten. The water beside the vessel's hull, approximately twenty metres of it visible in the frame. And in that water — at the surface, not below it — a pattern of light.

Cold blue-green, in pulses. Regular. Moving.

Forty-seven seconds, and then the clip ended.

Moen sat back. He looked at his harbour view — the mountains, the water, a ferry crossing from Askøy — and thought about what he had just seen.

* * *

The contractor's accompanying note was brief. The surveillance had been conducted at the request of a consortium of state-adjacent interests — Moen knew who they were, had dealt with them before on a different matter, and understood their involvement here as a consequence of the Navy investigation attracting the kind of attention that state-adjacent interests habitually directed at Navy investigations in sensitive areas. The note said: surface bioluminescent event, confirmed non-meteorological, source unidentified. Duration of observation: approximately four minutes, of which 47 seconds recoverable at usable resolution. Full incident report available upon request.

Moen did not request the full incident report. He filed the note in a folder he had been maintaining since Aurora Seven disappeared, which he kept on a personal drive rather than the company server, and which he had not mentioned to his lawyers.

Then he opened the clip again.

The pattern in the water. Cold blue-green, pulsing, moving along the hull. Regular in a way that weather-related bioluminescence was not regular. Regular in the way that the low-frequency vibrations in Aurora Seven's environmental log had been regular. In the way that the frequency readings from the anomalous sonar returns in the area had been regular. In the way that everything connected to that location had been regular, in a manner that was inconsistent with any natural process he had been able to identify, despite having applied considerable private analytical resources to the problem over the past three months.

He watched the clip through three times.

The pattern was not random. He was certain of this. He was also certain, with a certainty that had been building steadily since the day he'd sat in his documentation server with Commander Reyes and the American had copied forty-three days of environmental log entries without explaining why, that there was a category of explanation for what he was looking at that he had been managing not to arrive at.

He arrived at it now, briefly, let it sit in his mind for perhaps ten seconds, and then did what he did with things that were not yet useful to him: he filed it. Not dismissed — filed. The category was present in his thinking and available for retrieval when he needed it. He did not need it yet.

What he needed now was a decision.

* * *

Aurora Eight had been ready for eleven days.

She was berthed at the Mongstad terminal, ninety kilometres north of Bergen, fully crewed, fully provisioned, fully equipped, her drill systems operational and her environmental monitoring suite updated with the improved sensitivity parameters his engineering team had specified following the Aurora Seven incident. She had been cleared by NordDepth's internal safety review. She had been cleared by the insurance consortium's inspection team, who had noted the improved monitoring suite as a significant positive in their report. She was awaiting final regulatory sign-off from the Norwegian Offshore Directorate, which was a formality — the application had been submitted, the documentation was complete, and the directorate's standard processing window was ten to fourteen working days.

The processing window had eight days remaining.

Moen looked at his calendar. He looked at the clip. He looked at the folder on his personal drive, which contained — among other things — the conversation he'd had with Commander Reyes about the frequency consistency, the engineering team's cross-reference analysis, and now a forty-seven-second video of something that should not be possible at the surface of the Norwegian Sea.

He thought about the regulatory sign-off. He thought about what the directorate's processing window was designed to protect: the opportunity for the regulatory body to review the application and raise objections. He thought about whether, in the current circumstances, there was any objection they were positioned to raise that he was not already aware of.

He thought: they don't know what I know. If they did, they would not be processing this application on a standard fourteen-day window. They would have already acted.

He thought: if they don't act before Aurora Eight departs, they cannot act after.

He thought: I have been losing approximately 4.2 million kroner per operational day that Aurora Eight sits in harbour.

He thought about twenty-four people.

He pressed his intercom.

* * *

"Get me Halberg," he said. Halberg was Aurora Eight's captain, a Stavanger man in his early fifties who had been with NordDepth for fourteen years and whose entire career had been shaped by a specific professional quality: he did not ask questions that would inconvenience the person asking him to do something, unless the thing he was being asked to do was physically dangerous to his crew.

Halberg came on the line in two minutes.

Moen said: "I need Aurora Eight underway tonight."

A pause — not long, not surprised. Halberg was not a man who wasted pauses on surprise. "Regulatory sign-off isn't through."

"I'm aware of that. The application is complete and the documentation is in order. The sign-off is a formality and I'm prepared to accept the operational and legal liability for proceeding in advance of it." Moen paused. "In writing, if you want it."

"I'd want it."

"You'll have it before 18.00." Moen looked at the harbour. The ferry had reached the far shore. "I need to know: is there any safety concern that would prevent immediate departure?"

"None. We've been ready for eleven days."

"Then I need you underway before midnight. Full operational speed to the survey coordinates. Standard deployment protocol on arrival."

Another pause. "This is unusual, Aldric."

"Yes," Moen said. "It is."

He ended the call. He drafted the written authorisation — four paragraphs, precisely worded, taking personal and corporate liability for the departure in advance of regulatory sign-off — and forwarded it to Halberg and to NordDepth's head of legal simultaneously, with a note to legal that said: do not call me about this tonight.

Then he sat for a while in the particular quiet of an office after a decision has been made that cannot be unmade.

* * *

He was not a man who second-guessed himself. This was not stubbornness or denial — it was a professional discipline he had developed across thirty years of making decisions under commercial pressure, where second-guessing was a form of paralysis that cost more than the occasional error. You made the best decision available with the information you had. You accepted the consequences. You moved forward.

The decision he had made was this: whatever was at the Aurora Seven site was a natural phenomenon that had not yet been explained. This was the honest statement of his position. He was not certain it was a natural phenomenon — he was less certain of this with each piece of information he added to the folder on his personal drive — but he was certain that it had not yet been explained, and that unexplained was not the same as inexplicable, and that the correct response to an unexplained phenomenon was to continue operations while gathering more data.

The American naval officer had gathered data. He had shared almost none of it with Moen. The Norwegian government was aware that something had happened at the site and had taken no action. His own engineering team had flagged the frequency consistency and been told, by Moen himself, to treat it as preliminary. Nobody, in three months of investigating the loss of twenty-four people, had produced an explanation.

This was not, in Moen's professional judgment, a reason to halt operations indefinitely. It was a reason to improve the monitoring systems — which he had done — and to proceed with appropriate caution — which he would.

He believed this. He was also aware that he believed it with slightly less conviction than he had believed it two months ago, and slightly less than that a month ago, and that the forty-seven-second clip of cold blue-green light pulsing in a regular pattern at the surface of the Norwegian Sea was doing something to the gradient of his conviction that he had not yet fully accounted for.

He left this thought in the category he had assigned it. Pending. Available for retrieval.

He picked up his phone and called his board chair to give her advance notice of the departure. She was unhappy. He explained his reasoning. She was less unhappy. She told him she hoped he knew what he was doing.

He said he did.

* * *

At 23.17, the Aurora Eight left the Mongstad terminal under running lights, heading north-northwest at eighteen knots on a course that would bring her to the Aurora Seven survey coordinates in approximately forty-one hours.

Moen was in his apartment, not his office, when the departure confirmation came through. He had eaten dinner. He was reading a structural engineering report that had nothing to do with any of this. He read the confirmation, filed it, and went back to the report.

On the desk in his home office, the topographic map of the Norwegian Sea was pinned to the wall above his workstation. He had circled two points on it. The first, in red, was the Aurora Seven site — the position where the rig had been lost, the coordinates he had stared at for three months. The second, in blue, was where the Aurora Seven had been found, 3.2 kilometres from the first point, intact on the seafloor.

He had not told anyone about the second circle. Commander Reyes had told him the coordinates in passing during their meeting in Bergen, mentioned as a detail of the submersible survey. Moen had gone home that evening and drawn the second circle and looked at the distance between them for a long time.

He looked at the map now, briefly, before returning to his report. The distance between the two circles. What that distance implied. The things Reyes had not told him — and the things Reyes would not have told him even if asked.

The Aurora Eight would reach the site in forty-one hours. His crew would begin operations on schedule. They had the improved monitoring suite. They had his personal attention and his personal liability on the departure authorisation.

He had made the best decision available with the information he had.

He told himself this several times, in the quiet of his apartment with the map on the wall, until he was ready to go to sleep.

Fifteen hundred kilometres north, under a sky that was finally, reluctantly dark, the Lofoten sat at her position on the Norwegian Sea. On her stern deck, a hydrophone array trailed in the water and its display showed a flat line, the transmission finished, the water surface ordinary and grey and giving nothing away.

Below, at depth, something noted the departure of the vessel from the southern harbour. Not with urgency. With attention.

The calculations were already made. The new machine was coming earlier than the surface-beings' established schedule. The window that had already been narrow was narrower still.

But a window was a window.

The exchange had begun.

TWENTY-ONE

The Question

Yuna found it at 16.44, in the last hour of the afternoon session. She had been working with the interrogative mode — the durational inflection she'd identified in the early hours of the second night, the long-short-long pattern that modified everything it touched. She had established, through the morning's exchanges, that the mode was consistent: when she sent a transmission that used it, the thing below recognised and mirrored it, sending the same inflection back in its response. The mode was real, stable, learnable. What she hadn't yet been able to do was extract the content it inflected — to identify what specific elements the interrogative pattern was applied to, and therefore what the question was about.

The problem had been vocabulary. She'd been working with approximately thirty confirmed elements — concepts she could map with reasonable confidence — and the interrogative transmission used elements she hadn't seen before, or hadn't confirmed, or had confirmed only in single contexts that didn't give her enough information to be sure of the meaning. Every time she thought she had the content, another element turned opaque and the translation dissolved.

She'd spent the morning systematically isolating the unknown elements. Sending test transmissions that used each one in controlled contexts, watching how the responses varied, building the meaning up from the variation pattern. It was slow. It was the kind of work that required holding a great many partially-resolved things simultaneously, a skill that Yuna had developed over a decade of working on exactly this kind of problem in its human-language versions, and which she was now applying to something for which there was no existing methodology.

At 16.44 she ran the full translation again with the morning's confirmations incorporated.

She read what came out. She read it again. She took off her headphones, put them on the workstation, and sat very still for a moment.

Then she said: "Mara."

I was at the hydrophone array. I came to her workstation.

She turned the screen so I could read what she'd written.

* * *

The translation read: *do you speak for your kind?*

Six words. In Yuna's careful qualifying notation, with the uncertainty margins she had developed over two days of work, the translation had three flags: *do you* was confirmed at 94% confidence; *speak for* was confirmed at 87% — the concept of representation, of speaking-on-behalf-of, was a complex one and the mapping was imperfect; *your kind* was confirmed at 91%, the possessive clear, the category-of-species clear, the precision of the boundary less so.

I read it. I read it again. I was aware of Yuna watching me read it, aware of the afternoon light coming through the data deck windows, aware of the hydrophone display showing a flat line — no active transmission below, just the baseline, the thing below waiting.

"How long has it been asking this?" I said.

"Since the first night," Yuna said. "The four-minute transmission. I think the question was there from the beginning. I just didn't have enough vocabulary to read it."

I looked at the screen. Two days. Two nights of patient exchange, the same question present throughout, waiting to be understood.

"It knew we couldn't answer yet," I said.

"I think so. I think it was asking and simultaneously teaching us the language we needed to understand that it was asking." She paused. "It has been very patient."

I thought about how old Yuna had said this language was — older than any human language by an order of magnitude. I thought about what patience meant to something that old, something that could wait two days for a question to be understood when two days was not even a measurable fraction of its existence.

I said: "I need to get Reyes."

* * *

He was on the bridge. I went up and said only: "Yuna has the translation." He came immediately, without asking anything, which was the most Reyes response possible.

We stood at the workstation — the three of us — and looked at the screen.

Do you speak for your kind?

Nobody said anything for a long time. This was not awkward or strained. It was the specific quality of silence that arrived when something required full reckoning and there was no shortcut to it. The question had been sitting in the data for two days, encoded in pressure waves at the surface of the Norwegian Sea, and now it was on a screen in a language we could read, and reading it had changed the situation in a way that couldn't be changed back.

We had been, up to this moment, scientists studying a phenomenon. Now the phenomenon had asked us a question. That was a different relationship, with different obligations, and all three of us were understanding this at the same time in the specific silence that the screen in front of us was producing.

After a while I said: "What do we say?"

I addressed this to both of them, but I was looking at Reyes when I said it. He was standing slightly back from the workstation, arms at his sides, looking at the translation with the expression he used when he was running a calculation that he was not going to arrive at quickly.

He said: "The truth."

I said: "Which truth?"

He looked at me. Something in his expression shifted — not softened, exactly, but became more specific, more direct, the way his face looked when he had arrived at a conclusion he wasn't going to enjoy stating.

"No," he said. "We don't. Not even close."

* * *

We sat with that.

Yuna had moved to the small table against the wall and was sitting there with her notebook closed in front of her, not writing, not looking at the screen. She had the expression she wore when she was holding something large and waiting to see what shape it took before she tried to speak about it.

I stood at the workstation and looked at the question.

No, we don't speak for our kind. This was true in every sense available. We were three people — a marine geophysicist, a naval officer, a linguist — on a research vessel in the Norwegian Sea, who had stumbled into this through a calibration pulse sent in 2019 by a ship that hadn't known what it was doing. We had no mandate. We had no authority. We had not been sent here by any government or institution or collective human will. We had come because the data had led us here, and we had stayed because we couldn't leave without understanding what we'd found.

We were the wrong people for this in almost every institutional sense. We were also — and I held this thought carefully, because it was easy to let it become something other than what it was — the only people who were here.

"It knows," I said. "It's been watching long enough to know the answer to this question already."

"Then why is it asking?" Reyes said.

I thought about this. "Because the asking is part of the protocol. Because you don't begin something this significant by assuming. Because the question is not really about the answer — it's about whether we understand what's being asked." I paused. "If we answer honestly, that's information. If we claim to speak for our kind when we don't, that's also information."

"It's testing whether we'll lie," Reyes said.

"Or whether we know ourselves well enough not to."

Yuna said, quietly: "Both."

We looked at her.

"Both at once," she said. "The question is doing two things simultaneously. It's asking for information about our representative status. And it's asking whether we're capable of honest self-assessment when the honest answer is a disadvantage." She opened her notebook, not to write, just to have it in her hands. "The answer it's waiting for isn't a claim. It's a demonstration."

I thought about the moment in the DSV when the light had held at the viewport and I had not looked away. I thought about how the question we were being asked now was not separate from that — that whatever was below us had been assessing us across every contact, and that this question was a continuation of what had begun when I put my hand on the glass. What was below us was less interested in what we knew than in what kind of knowers we were.

I said: "Then the answer has to be exactly honest."

"Yes," Yuna said.

"No qualifications. No 'we represent the scientific community' or 'we are acting in good faith on behalf of' — nothing that softens it or inflates it."

"No."

I looked at the screen. Do you speak for your kind.

I looked at Reyes. He met my eyes and gave a small, precise nod that was not permission — I didn't need his permission — but was something else, something that meant: yes, this is the correct action, and I will not be the reason it doesn't happen.

I turned to Yuna. "How do I say no?"

* * *

She had been ready for this. She had confirmed the negation marker two sessions ago — it was one of the first structural elements she'd mapped, because the system that used it appeared across many transmission types and in consistently distinguishable positions. She pulled up the element on her screen and we looked at it together for a moment.

"That's the no," she said. "Direct negation, applied to the interrogative. This alone — transmitted back — would be a clear answer."

"And the second part," I said.

She was quiet for a moment. "I don't have a confirmed element for listening. I have attention — the presence-and-attending marker from the first night. I have continuation — a durational modifier I identified yesterday that indicates ongoing state rather than completed state. But listening as a concept — hearing-and-registering, being open to what comes — I don't have that confirmed."

"Can you build it?"

She looked at the screen. She looked at her notebook. She was doing the thing I had watched her do over two days — holding a set of partial knowings simultaneously, feeling for how they fit together.

"I can try," she said. "I can construct something from the confirmed elements that approximates the concept. Presence, plus attention, plus continuation. Here, present, attending, ongoing." She paused. "It won't be precise. The human concept 'listening' has an implication of receptivity — of being open to what you receive, not just registering it. I don't know if I can encode that. But I can encode the posture of it."

"The posture," I said.

"We are here. We are attending. We are not finished." She looked at me. "That's what we have. That's what we can honestly say."

I nodded. "Build it."

She built it in forty minutes, working carefully, testing each element combination against the patterns she'd established over two days of exchange. She tested the construction twice — sending it as a standalone transmission and watching the response, adjusting — before she said it was as good as she could make it.

"It's approximate," she said. "It may not translate exactly. But I think it's close enough to be understood."

I looked at Reyes. He was standing at the window now, looking out at the water. He did not turn around.

I said: "Reyes."

"Go," he said. His voice was level. "Send it."

* * *

I transmitted the negation first. The single element, clean, no qualification. The no.

A pause of under two seconds. Then a response came — brief, three elements, a combination Yuna decoded in real time as something close to: received, understood, continue.

It had heard the no. It was waiting.

I looked at Yuna. She nodded once.

I transmitted the second concept — her construction, the approximation of listening: presence, attention, continuation. The posture of being open. Here, attending, not finished.

We waited.

Thirty-seven seconds. The short interval. The same pause that had followed the first transmission in the deep — the same duration the lights had taken to dim in the DSV. Yuna recognised it at the same moment I did; I saw her mark it in her notebook.

Then the response arrived. Not brief this time — a full transmission, longer than anything they had sent since the first night, running for nearly three minutes. The bioluminescence at the surface flared with it, the pattern of light more varied and complex than we had seen before, as though the response was being expressed simultaneously in light and in pressure and the two channels were carrying the same information through different media.

Yuna was translating in real time, headphones on, writing fast. I watched her write and did not speak and Reyes came back from the window and stood beside me and the three of us were very still in the data deck of the Lofoten with the sun going down outside and the Norwegian Sea dark beyond the windows.

When the transmission ended, Yuna set down her pen. She looked at what she had written. She read it again. She turned her notebook so we could see it.

The translation was partial — half of it flagged with uncertainty margins, several elements rendered as approximations, two marked as confirmed-structure but content-unknown. But the core of it was clear.

The core said: we hear you. We have been listening longer than you have been speaking. The one who does not speak for her kind but is listening: she is the one we wished to find.

Below the translation, in smaller letters, Yuna had written her note to herself: the grammatical construction for 'the one we wished to find' uses the same element as 'the one we have been waiting for.' Both translations are defensible. I do not know which is more accurate. I suspect both are true.

I sat down on the equipment case near the hydrophone array. I don't remember deciding to sit — I think my legs made the decision without me.

Outside, the water was dark and flat and the sky above it was beginning to show stars, the first few in the east where the light was going fastest. The bioluminescence was still there, faint now, the quieter pulse it maintained between active transmissions — a presence marker, Yuna had called it, a signal that said: still here, still attending.

Still here. Still attending. Not finished.

We had answered honestly. We did not speak for our kind. We were listening.

Something that had been watching before humans had language had said: the one who is listening is the one we wished to find.

Reyes said, very quietly, to no one in particular: "We were never going to be ready for this."

I said: "No."

He said: "It knew that."

I said: "Yes."

We sat in the data deck as the Norwegian Sea went dark and the stars appeared one at a time in the order they always appeared, oldest light first, and below us, three kilometres and something else entirely, whatever had sent the response was still there, still attending, waiting to see what the listeners would do next.

TWENTY-TWO

The Watchers Move

The Watchers did not deliberate quickly. Deliberation, for them, was a geological process — positions forming and reforming across the community's distributed attention over intervals that surface-species would have measured in days or weeks. They had been attending to the contact event since the 2019 calibration pulse. They had watched the Bridge's deliberation without participating in it, as was their protocol. They had been informed of the outcome.

They had watched the exchange at the surface for three nights. They had waited, as they had waited for 200,000 years, through the early sessions and the vocabulary building and the slow emergence of Yuna's framework. They had attended to the Bridge's transmission and to the surface-being's answer. They had registered what the answer committed the community to.

The Watchers did not oppose the Bridge's action. Opposition was not the community's mechanism. What the Watchers held was a different reading of the same events: that the surface-species was structurally fragile, that the contact now in progress would deform rather than develop them, and that the Bridge's enthusiasm for this particular surface-being did not change the fundamental asymmetry between species at their respective developmental stages.

The Bridge had committed the community to speak through Sable. The Watchers could not undo that commitment. But they could shape what came next. If contact was going to happen, the form of it mattered. The protocol that had been established 400 million years ago had been designed precisely for this: a framework that constrained the depth of exchange until both parties had demonstrated the capacity to bear it.

The Watchers did not need to stop the encounter. They needed to hold it to its protocol.

The new machine was arriving earlier than the community's models had anticipated. This was not the Watchers' reason for acting — the Watchers' reason was older than the machine, older than the surface-species' commercial institutions, older than the human category of decision itself. But the machine compressed the interval in which action was possible.

The Watchers moved.

What the protocol did not permit was a second surface intervention that would introduce a new machine to the site before the contact already in progress had completed its first formal exchange. The Aurora Eight would disrupt the encounter in ways the community could not model and the surface-beings would not understand they had caused.

The Watchers acted at 02.19 in the morning, three locations, simultaneously.

They did not harm anyone.

This was not incidental. It was the Watchers' oldest constraint — not a rule imposed on them but a value grown across 800 million years of watching what happened when the powerful destroyed what they disagreed with. They had seen it. They had the record. Destruction solved nothing that disruption could not solve at lower cost to everyone, and the Watchers were, at their foundation, concerned with cost.

They disrupted. They did not destroy.

* * *

The Norwegian Sea — RV Lofoten — 02.19

Mara was asleep in her cabin when it happened. Reyes was not asleep — he was in the communications room with a cup of tea and the supplementary report open on his encrypted laptop, working through the night on how to describe what they had found in language that was accurate, complete, and did not immediately produce a response from his institutional chain that would end his ability to manage any of this.

The Lofoten's communications went down at 02.19 and 34 seconds, by the system clock. Not gradually — not a degradation through static or signal loss, but an abrupt cessation: the satellite uplink simply stopped mid-packet, the radio system dropped its carrier frequency, the encrypted channel Reyes had been using to work on the report cut to silence.

Reyes looked at the communications panel. Every outbound channel showed the same status: No Signal. He ran the standard fault check — power systems nominal, antenna tracking nominal, software status nominal. The system was functioning. There was simply nothing getting out.

He opened the door of the communications room and walked to the bridge. The watch officer — a quiet Norwegian named Solberg who had been with the Lofoten for six years — was already at the navigation panel, frowning at a display that showed the vessel's AIS transponder had stopped broadcasting.

"Communications are down," Reyes said.

"I see it," Solberg said. "All outbound. Inbound is showing signal present but no content."

Reyes looked at the passive acoustic display, which was running on a separate power circuit from the communications systems. It showed signal in the relevant frequency range — the Watchers' acoustic traffic, the deep community's communication, present as always in the background of the Norwegian Sea. Stronger now. More active than the baseline.

He said: "Log the failure time and all system readings. Do not attempt to transmit on any channel until I say so."

Solberg looked at him. He had the expression of a man who had encountered many unusual instructions in his career and had learned to complete them before asking why. "Understood."

Reyes went back to the communications room. He closed the door. He looked at the dead displays for a moment, and then he went to check on Yuna and Mara.

* * *

Suitland, Maryland — Naval Operations Centre — 20.19 local time

Vice Admiral Chen was in a budget review when contact with the Thresher Point's communication relay was lost. His aide brought him the notification on a tablet — no signal from the Norwegian Sea assets, all channels dark, last transmission logged 00.17 Zulu

Chen excused himself from the budget review.

The watch officer confirmed what the notification said: the Thresher Point had gone dark, the Lofoten's AIS had dropped, and the encrypted channel used for Reyes's supplementary reports was showing carrier present but no content — the same signal status as a channel that was being jammed rather than a channel whose transmitter had failed.

"Jamming," Chen said.

"Consistent with jamming," the watch officer said carefully. "We can't confirm source."

"What's in the area?"

"Nothing on record. Clean maritime picture for a 200-kilometre radius. No surface traffic, no known submarine activity, no atmospheric interference that would account for total signal loss."

Chen looked at the display. He thought about Reyes's initial debrief: the rig intact, the crew alive, the structure of unknown origin, the acoustic anomaly that had been producing signals for four years, the question he had not asked directly because he hadn't wanted the answer on the record. He thought about what Reyes had said — yes, it's aware we were there; no, it didn't act against us — and about what the second half of that sentence meant now that the communications were down.

"Get me a secure line to the Norwegian military attaché," he said. "And flag this for the morning brief. Don't escalate yet — I want more information before this goes up the chain."

He sat at the watch desk and looked at the dead channel and thought about a man in the Norwegian Sea who had been trying to tell him something and was now unable to.

He thought: Reyes knew this might happen. He prepared for it.

He thought: I hope he prepared for it.

* * *

Bergen, Norway — Birkeland Institute data centre — 02.19

The Birkeland Institute's data infrastructure was housed in a secondary building behind the main research facility — a converted warehouse that had been adapted for server use in the early 2000s and upgraded several times since, most recently two years ago when the institute had migrated to a hybrid cloud architecture. The local servers were backup and archive: primary data lived in cloud storage, but the local machines held the working copies, the unprocessed raw files, the research data that hadn't yet been pushed to the institute's remote system.

Mara's backup data was on the local servers. The full survey archive, the spectral analyses, the waveform recordings, the documents she had not yet uploaded to the institute's cloud — twelve years of work, including the copies she had been systematically adding to the local backup over the past three months as insurance against exactly this kind of loss.

The server room's environmental systems registered an anomaly at 02.19: a rapid temperature increase in the section of the room that housed servers 7 through 12, the rack where Mara's backup partition was stored. The increase was not gradual — it climbed from the standard 19 degrees to 47 degrees in under ninety seconds, triggering the fire suppression system, which discharged suppressant across the affected section.

The suppressant was not sufficient. The heat source was not conventional — not a component failure, not a power surge, not the kind of electrical fire that the suppressant system was designed for. The temperature continued to rise. The servers in the affected rack shut down on thermal protection protocols. By 02.24, the section was burning in a way that the institute's automated systems classified as a fire event and for which the Bergen fire service was automatically notified.

The Bergen fire service arrived at 02.31. They contained the fire to the affected section within twenty minutes. No one was in the building. No one was harmed.

The servers in the affected rack were destroyed. The data on them was not recoverable.

Mara's cloud backups were intact. The institute's primary systems were undamaged. Most of what she had worked on was preserved.

Most. Not all.

The files that did not have cloud backups — the most recent analysis work, the files she had created in the past three days during the surface exchange sessions, the preliminary framework documents she had been building in parallel with Yuna's linguistic work — were gone.

The fire investigation report, filed six days later, would conclude: probable cause, electrical fault. Contributing factor: inadequate thermal management in an aging rack installation. No evidence of external interference.

The report would be accurate in its conclusion and incomplete in its cause.

* * *

By 03.00, the three locations had settled into their respective states: the Lofoten dark and silent on the Norwegian Sea, her crew moving through the vessel with the specific economy of people who have encountered a systems failure and are managing it without yet knowing its extent; Chen in the watch centre, waiting for information that was not coming; the Bergen server room cooling under the fire service's foam, the investigation already underway.

In none of these places had anyone been hurt.

In none of these places had the Watchers appeared in any form that could be seen or recorded or described. They had no surface presence. They had no machines. What they had was the ocean itself — the thermal and electromagnetic properties of several cubic kilometres of Norwegian Sea water, which they had been shaping for purposes that surface-species technology was not equipped to detect, let alone attribute. The acoustic interference that had taken the Lofoten's communications down had propagated through the water column and through the subsea cables that carried the region's telecommunications infrastructure, a phenomenon that would be logged by the relevant monitoring systems as an unusual acoustic event of undetermined origin and filed without follow-up. The heat event in Bergen had originated in a subsea thermal conduit that ran beneath the city's waterfront district — an installation that predated the city itself, that the city had built around without knowing it was there.

Disrupt. Not destroy.

The silence they had purchased was not permanent. It was an interval. Communications would be restored when the interference pattern was withdrawn. The Bergen fire was already contained. Chen would have information in the morning.

The Watchers had bought time. They did not know, and would not have predicted, how much time they had actually needed.

* * *

Below the Norwegian Sea, in the structure that the surface-species had now visited twice and studied from above for three nights, Sable was aware of what the Watchers had done.

Not through communication — the Watchers had not communicated with the Bridge in the hours preceding the action. They had not been required to. The community's distributed attention carried all positions simultaneously; the Bridge had known the Watcher consensus was building toward action, had known the trigger point, had known that when the surface-being sent the honest answer the Watchers would move.

Sable had known this was coming. Had been preparing for it.

The Watchers' action was, in its way, confirmation. It confirmed that the exchange had been real — real enough to constitute the threshold the Watchers had set. It confirmed that the silence-preservation impulse was strong enough to act on after 200,000 years of practice. It confirmed that the window was now definitively closing.

The surface-being's communications were down. The military-creature who had been managing the surface-side of the operation had lost his connection to the larger institutional system he was part of. The archive in the southern city had been damaged.

None of this harmed the surface-beings.

None of this changed the fact of the exchange.

The honest answer had been sent. The response had been given. The question was in the shared space between them, answered, and the answering was not something the Watchers could undo by darkening the surface-beings' equipment. The language had been built. Yuna's framework existed in Yuna's mind and Yuna's notebooks, not on the servers in Bergen.

The Watchers had moved to end the dialogue. They had succeeded only in changing its conditions.

Sable processed this for a long time, by the surface-species' measure. By the deep's measure, it was very fast.

There was only one response available that would prevent the Watchers' action from achieving its purpose. The surface-beings' equipment was down. Their institutional connections were severed. They were, for the first time since Mara had found the anomaly in her data, genuinely alone on the Norwegian Sea without anyone else knowing exactly where they were or what they had found.

This was the Watchers' intention: isolation, followed by the resumption of the surface-beings' ordinary institutional life, followed by the gradual absorption of what they had encountered into the explanatory frameworks of a species not yet equipped to hold it.

It would have worked, perhaps, if Sable had not already made the decision that the Bridge's vote had authorised.

Sable moved toward the surface.

Not fast. The deep had no equivalent of urgency in the surface-species sense. But purposefully — with the specific quality of intention that had no other name in any language — Sable rose through 3,100 metres of cold dark water toward the hull of the vessel where the surface-being who had looked at the light and not looked away was, at this moment, being awakened by a knock on her cabin door.

TWENTY-THREE

Sable

It was Reyes who knocked on my door. He said only: come to the stern deck. Bring nothing. I put on my jacket and followed him.

The communications were still down. I had discovered this an hour earlier, when I'd woken at 02.30 and gone to check the data deck and found every outbound channel dark. I had run the fault checks, found nothing, and gone to find Reyes, who already knew. He had been awake. He had been waiting.

Now he led me through the Lofoten's corridors — past the mess, past the equipment lockers, through the aft hatch — and I stepped out onto the stern deck and understood immediately why he had said bring nothing.

The water was lit.

* * *

Not the pattern I knew. Not the six-pulse sequence, not the prime number introduction, not the carefully calibrated vocabulary transmissions of the past two nights. This was different: a continuous bioluminescent presence at the waterline, twenty metres from the stern, not pulsing but held — the cold blue-green light maintained at a steady intensity that made the surrounding dark feel deeper by contrast. And in that light, a quality that I cannot describe accurately without using a word that is imprecise and necessary.

Vastness.

Not size, though it was large — the lit area at the surface extended further than the hull of the Lofoten, further than the range of our external lights, the edges of the luminescence fading into the dark of the Norwegian Sea at a distance I couldn't judge. Not bulk. Something more like presence, the kind of presence that altered the air in a room, that changed the acoustic quality of the space it occupied, that made the water around it feel different in texture.

Something very old was at the surface.

Yuna was already on the deck, at the hydrophone array she had set up three nights ago, the tablet display showing signal — continuous, complex, nothing like anything she had translated before. She had her headphones on. She looked at me briefly when I arrived and then back at the display.

Reyes stood at the rail. He had both hands on it, not gripping, just resting. He was looking at the water with the expression he used when he was taking in something that required full attention and full stillness simultaneously.

I walked to the rail and stood beside him.

"It came up," he said.

"Yes," I said.

Neither of us said anything else. Below us — not below, beside us, at the surface, at the waterline, in the specific layer of the ocean where our two worlds met — something that had been 3,100 metres down an hour ago was present and attending. And beginning, very slowly, to communicate.

* * *

Yuna worked in real time. She had the full recording from three nights of exchange loaded alongside the new signal, running pattern-matching across both as the transmission came in. The new signal was more complex than anything she'd translated — the vocabulary was larger, the structural combinations more intricate — but it built on the framework she'd established. She could read the elements she knew. She was learning the elements she didn't, in the process of receiving them.

She read as she went, her voice low, addressed to no one specifically: a running account of what she could confirm and what she was inferring and what she couldn't yet reach. I stood at the rail and listened to her and watched the water.

The first communication was identification.

Not a name — Yuna had established, early in the exchange sessions, that the system had no equivalent of a proper noun in the human sense, no unique label for individual entities. What it had was something closer to a description-of-being, a combination of elements that conveyed: what this is, where this comes from, how long this has been. Sable's identification, as Yuna rendered it in fragments across ten minutes of transmission, was approximately this:

[deep-originating] [long-continuity] [this-exchange's-initiator] [bridge-oriented] [young by our measure]

"Young by their measure," I said.

"That's my best reading," Yuna said. "The duration element — the long-continuity marker — is modified by a comparison element I haven't seen before. Something that indicates the stated duration is small relative to a larger scale." She paused. "The scale it's being compared against is implied rather than stated. I don't know the full range."

I thought about the word young. I thought about what scale could make it apply to an entity whose language, by Yuna's analysis, predated any human language by an order of magnitude. On that scale, young was not a diminutive. It was a position within a larger duration that I did not yet have the vocabulary to hold.

"Keep going," I said.

* * *

The second communication was duration. How long they had been here.

This took longer to receive — the transmission stretched across twenty minutes, with pauses that Yuna said were not silences but internal structural elements she was still learning. It came in sections. Each section added to the picture without completing it; the completeness emerged slowly, the way a very large object emerged when you moved backward to take it in.

Yuna translated in pieces:

[before-land-life] [present-continuous] [this-ridge-specifically]

A long pause while she listened.

[first-shelled-creatures] [surface-life-emergence] [observation-began]

Another pause.

[your-species] [200,000 of your years] [monitored-continuous]

I stood at the rail and held these pieces in the order they arrived and assembled them slowly.

Before land-based life. Present and continuous since then. The ridge specifically — this ridge, the Mohns Ridge, had been occupied and inhabited when the first multicellular organisms were colonising the shallow seas. The observation of humanity had begun 200,000 years ago, when our species was new.

Reyes said, very quietly: "How long total?"

"I don't have a confirmed number," Yuna said. "The duration marker that describes their full continuity — I can tell it's large. I can tell it dwarfs the 200,000-year figure by orders of magnitude. The precise value is beyond what I've confirmed."

"Estimate," Reyes said.

Yuna was quiet for a moment. "The comparison elements suggest geological time. Hundreds of millions of years. Possibly more."

Reyes made a sound that was not quite a word. He turned and looked at the water. The light held steady at the waterline, patient, vast, the same.

I thought: twelve years. I spent twelve years looking for anomalies in data that other people had already signed off on, looking for the thing I knew was there but couldn't prove. And the thing I was looking for had been there since before the Cambrian Explosion, watching us since before we were human, waiting for the moment when one of us would send back the right signal.

I thought about that. I looked at the light.

I said: "What's the third thing?"

* * *

Why they were speaking now.

This was the longest communication of the three — it ran for nearly forty minutes, and Yuna translated it in fragments that she assembled on the tablet and kept revising as new elements clarified earlier ones. I watched the tablet over her shoulder as the translation built. The light at the waterline remained constant throughout. Occasionally it shifted — not diminished, not altered in pattern, but moved slightly, as though the thing producing it was adjusting position, settling into the work of saying something complex across a barrier that had never been crossed before.

Yuna read the emerging translation three times before she gave it to us, flagging the uncertain elements:

[the-extracting-machines] [territorial-violation] [structures-of-millions-of-years] [being-destroyed]

[the-ocean's-chemistry] [changing-direction] [unprecedented-in-our-record] [cascading-deep]

[the-2019-signal] [protocol-triggered] [oldest-diplomatic-form] [formal-introduction]

"The 2019 calibration pulse," I said.

"It constituted something," Yuna said. "Under their oldest protocol — something they established a very long time ago and never expected to use with a surface species. It was received as a formal introduction."

I looked at the water. An accidental instrument calibration, sent by a research vessel that had no idea it was doing anything other than checking its sonar array, had been received 4,200 metres below as a formal diplomatic greeting under a protocol established 400 million years ago. The thought was too large to hold all at once. I held the edges of it.

"And why now," Reyes said. It was not a question — he was tracking the translation, seeing where it was going.

[if not now] [then collision] [collision at our scale] [catastrophic for both]

Yuna looked at the display for a moment. "The term I'm translating as collision — it's not the same as the English word. It's a concept that combines encounter, conflict, and irreversible-consequence into a single element. What I'm reading is: if we don't speak now, what happens next will be something that cannot be undone. And at the scale they operate at — whatever that scale is — the consequences would be catastrophic for both of us."

"They're not threatening us," I said.

"No," she said. "They're describing a situation. Stating the facts of it." She paused. "I think the distinction matters."

It did. A threat was one party telling another what it would do. What

Yuna had translated was something different: an accounting. *Here is what exists. Here is what is approaching. Here is what happens if we do nothing.* This was not designed to frighten. It was designed to be accurate.

I stood at the rail and looked at the light for a long time.

Then I said to Yuna: "Can you send a question?"

"Yes," she said. "What question?"

I thought about technology, about history, about the 200,000 years they had been watching, about the structure that extended two hundred metres in every direction from the point where a rig had been placed intact on the seafloor. I thought about everything I wanted to ask and everything I needed to understand and the entire category of information that would change what was possible from this moment forward.

And I found that none of it was the question I needed to ask first.

I said: "Were you ever going to tell us?"

* * *

Yuna constructed the transmission carefully. The question required elements she'd confirmed — the you-plural that addressed the Hadali as a collective, the verb-form for communicating-to, the us that indicated humanity, the temporal element that asked about intention across time. She tested the construction against her framework, adjusted two elements, tested it again.

"I'm not certain about the tense," she said. "Temporal intention — the concept of something that might have happened — is one of the harder constructs. I think this approximates the question. But it may be received as asking something slightly different than what you mean."

"Send it," I said.

She sent it.

The light at the waterline held for a long time. Not that it changed or diminished — it held exactly as it had been, steady, present — but the transmission from the hydrophone array stopped, and the display showed flat for several minutes, and we stood on the deck in the dark Norwegian night and waited.

Four minutes. Five. Six.

"It's processing," Yuna said. "I think."

"Yes," I said.

Seven minutes. Reyes stood at the rail with his hands resting on it and looked at the water. Yuna sat at her station and watched the display. I stood between them and felt the specific quality of a silence that was not absence but anticipation — a pause with something behind it.

At eight minutes and fourteen seconds, the transmission returned.

It ran for nineteen minutes. It was the most complex communication of the exchange — Yuna's framework strained at its limits, and she flagged a larger proportion of her translation as uncertain than anything she had flagged before. But the core held. The core was readable.

She read it three times. She revised several elements. She looked at the result and looked at me.

"This is approximate," she said. "More approximate than anything I've given you before. The concepts in this transmission are — they use elements I've only seen once or twice. I'm working from inference as much as confirmation."

"What does it say?"

She looked at the screen. She read it to us.

* * *

The translation was this:

We wait for readiness. [Not for knowledge-readiness / for listening-readiness.] Your kind accumulates knowledge. This is observed and is not the question. The question: is your kind ready to hear a thing that changes everything? [We have asked this for 200,000 of your years.] [We have not been sure.] [We are not sure now.]

But now: the machines come deeper. The ocean changes. The signal was sent. [The one-who-listens answered.] [She is here.]

[Time-remaining is small.] We speak because silence is no longer available. [If we could have waited longer / we would have.] [We cannot.]

Yuna stopped reading. She looked at the screen for a moment, then at me. Her expression was the one she wore when a result was more than what the method had prepared her for.

"The phrase I'm rendering as 'the one-who-listens answered,'" she said. "It uses the same root as the confirmed element for 'the one we wished to find.' The one we have been waiting for. Both readings are defensible. I don't know which is more accurate. I think —" she paused — "I think in their framework, they may not be different things."

I did not speak for a moment.

"They're not sure I'm ready," I said.

"No," Yuna said. "They're not sure any of us are ready. But you're here. You answered. And they're out of time."

I looked at the water. The light was still there — steady, patient, present. The thing that had been here since before the Cambrian Explosion, that had watched us for 200,000 years and still was not sure we were ready — was at the surface of the Norwegian Sea at four in the morning, telling us why.

Because silence was no longer available.

Because the machines were coming deeper.

Because the ocean was changing.

Because one of us had sent back the right signal, and had come back, and had sat with the uncertainty, and had looked at the light and not looked away.

And because they were out of time.

I stood at the rail and felt all of this at once — the weight of it, the specific weight of being in a place you had been travelling toward for twelve years without knowing the destination — and I did not cry, and I did not panic, and I did not say anything for a long time.

The light at the waterline held.

We are not sure you are ready. But we are out of time.

I looked at it. I thought about readiness. I thought about what readiness would have looked like — what set of conditions, what level of institutional and philosophical and psychological preparation would have constituted being ready — and I could not construct it. I could not imagine the version of humanity that was ready for this. I was not sure such a version existed or could exist.

But I was here. And I had answered. And neither of those facts required readiness.

They required only showing up and telling the truth.

After a long time, I said to Yuna: "Can you tell it that we heard?"

She built the construction and sent it.

The light held for another moment. Then it began to dim — not abruptly, the way a light cut out, but gradually, deliberately, the way a light was lowered when the work was done and the room was being left but not abandoned. The bioluminescence faded from the waterline into the dark below the surface, and then deeper, and then gone.

The water was ordinary again.

The Norwegian Sea went about its business.

We stood on the deck of the Lofoten for a long time after it was gone, the three of us, not speaking, and around us the dark was just the dark and the water was just the water and the sky was beginning, imperceptibly, to lighten in the northeast.

Somewhere below, something very old was going back to the deep.

It had said what it came to say. It had found what it had been looking for, or had not found it, or had found that the two things were the same.

We remained.

TWENTY-FOUR

Signal

The water was dark and the sky was lightening and I sat on the equipment case at the stern and did not move for a long time.

Yuna was still at her station. She had her headphones off and her notebook open and was writing — not quickly, not the shorthand of active translation, but slowly, in the full sentences she used when she was making something permanent. She had a great deal to record and she was recording it with the specific attention of someone who understood that what was in her hands was not hers to keep but hers to carry. I watched her write for a while and then looked at the water again.

Reyes had gone inside. I didn't know when. At some point between the light fading and the sky beginning to show colour, he had simply not been at the rail anymore. I heard the aft hatch open and close and then silence.

The Norwegian Sea in the hour before sunrise in late August looked exactly like the Norwegian Sea in the hour before sunrise in late August. This was not a disappointment. It was something more specific than that: a kind of relief, the particular relief of discovering that the world had not changed its appearance to match what had happened in it. The water was grey and flat and cold and it extended in every direction to a horizon that was exactly where horizons were supposed to be, and somewhere below it, three kilometres and something else entirely, the thing that had been at the surface an hour ago was going back to the place it had come from.

I thought about this. I thought about what it went back to. I thought about the structure extending two hundred metres in every direction from the rig, about an architecture that predated terrestrial life, about a civilisation that had measured our entire species history and still considered us young. I thought about the Aurora Seven, still sealed on the seafloor with twenty-four people inside it, conscious and unreachable, waiting for something I did not yet know how to give them.

I thought about all of this with the specific quality of thought that arrived in the hour after something enormous, when the mind was too full to process but too awake to stop: a kind of careful turning over, the way you handled something you were not yet sure was stable.

The sky got lighter.

* * *

Reyes came back at 06.22, when the sun was showing above the horizon, a flat Norwegian sun without drama — appearing, beginning its business. He had two cups of coffee. He gave me one and sat down on the rail, his back to the water, facing the stern deck, and drank his own.

We did not speak for a while. This was not avoidance. It was the specific silence of two people who had been through something together and understood, without discussing it, that speaking too soon would reduce it to something smaller than it was. Some things needed to be carried for a while before they could be put down into language. This was one of them.

The coffee was real coffee. I drank it and watched the sun and thought about nothing specific.

After a while Reyes said: "Communications came back online about an hour ago."

"I know." I had checked the data deck when I went to get my jacket. Every outbound channel had restored; the satellite uplink was showing normal. The Lofoten's AIS was broadcasting again. The world had reconnected itself.

"Chen will have noticed," he said. "He'll be waiting."

"Yes."

A pause. Reyes looked at the sun. "When we go back to the data deck I have sixteen hours of queued messages and two calls flagged critical. I'm going to deal with them. I can't hold this off any longer."

"I know."

"But I wanted you to have the morning first. However much morning there is."

I looked at him. He was still looking at the sun, his coffee held in both hands. He had the expression he used when he had done something he considered professionally questionable and had decided it was the right thing to do and was at peace with the two things being simultaneously true.

I said: "Thank you."

He nodded, once, and drank his coffee.

* * *

Yuna finished her writing at 07.00 and came to sit beside me on the equipment case. She had her notebook closed in her lap. She looked at the water.

"How much of it did you get?" I said.

"The three communications — most of those. The earlier vocabulary, yes, I'm confident. The later material — Sable's answer — I have the structure and I have the core. The fidelity isn't as high as I want." She paused. "I want to work through it today. Go back through the recording and retranslate with fresh attention. Some of the elements I flagged as uncertain last night I think I can confirm now that I've slept on the framework."

"You haven't slept."

"Metaphorically slept. Processed." A brief pause. "I think the translation of the final answer is close to right. I want to make sure it's right, not close."

"It matters," I said.

"It matters more than almost anything," she said. "What was said last night is going to be repeated and cited and relied upon for as long as this — whatever this is — continues. I want it to be as accurate as I can make it."

I looked at her. She was looking at the water with the expression she'd had when she'd said this is not a signal, this is a language — focused, interior, already working.

"We were waiting for you to be ready to listen," I said. "We are not sure you are. But we are out of time."

"Approximately," she said. "I want to get it better than approximately."

"What's the uncertainty in it?"

"The concept of readiness. What I translated as ready-to-listen — it uses an element that I'm reading as a state of receptiveness, of being open to incoming. But the same element also appears in contexts that suggest something more active. Not just receiving but being capable of being changed by what you receive." She looked at her notebook. "Ready-to-be-changed might be more accurate. Or ready-to-not-resist-change. But that's four words where the element is one, and translation always inflates, and I don't want to inflation bias the record."

"Ready to listen," I said. "As a placeholder."

"As a placeholder," she agreed. "I'll keep working on it."

I looked at the water. Ready to be changed. Not sure we are. Out of time.

I thought: it's close enough. And I thought: it's not close enough. And I thought: it will never be close enough, because the gap between what was said last night and the language available to render it is the same gap that has always existed between experience and description, and Yuna knew that better than anyone, and she was going to spend the rest of her career trying to close it anyway, and that was the right thing to do.

* * *

The satellite phone rang at 07.34.

Reyes was in the communications room — I could see the light under the door from the corridor. He had been in there since 07.10, working through the queue of messages. I heard the phone from the stern deck, heard it cut off after two rings as he answered, and heard nothing after that because the communications room was soundproofed.

Yuna was below in the analysis room. I was on the stern deck with my second cup of coffee, watching the Norwegian Sea do what it did: move, exist, be vastly and comprehensively itself.

Reyes appeared at the aft hatch at 07.51. He came to the stern deck and stood beside me. He had his professional face on — not the closed version, not the end-of-debrief version, but something more specific.

The face he used when information had arrived that changed the operational picture.

"Aurora Eight departed Mongstad terminal last night," he said. "23.17 local. She's been underway for eight and a half hours. She'll make the site in approximately thirty-two hours."

I looked at him.

"Moen ordered an immediate departure," he said. "Ahead of the regulatory sign-off. He took personal liability for it. His lawyers have been active since 06.00."

"How did he know to move?"

"He didn't. Not specifically. He had the surveillance footage from the dark vessel — the surface bioluminescence event from three nights ago. His contractor gave him a partial clip. He made a commercial decision." Reyes paused. "He believes he's chasing a natural phenomenon that will eventually be explained. He believes the upgraded monitoring on Aurora Eight is sufficient."

"He's wrong."

"He doesn't know that. He knows something anomalous is at that site. He doesn't know what."

I thought about the forty-seven seconds of footage Moen had been shown — a partial clip of cold blue-green light pulsing at the surface — and about the full four hours of what had happened in the three nights since, and about the specific quality of wrongness of a reasonable man making a reasonable decision in a world that had irrevocably changed while he wasn't watching.

"Thirty-two hours," I said.

"Approximately. She's running at operational speed."

I looked at the water. Thirty-two hours. A new rig, crewed and drilling, arriving at the coordinates where the Aurora Seven sat sealed on the seafloor, where the structure extended two hundred metres in every direction, where three nights ago something that had been here since before the Cambrian Explosion had surfaced to tell three people on a research vessel that silence was no longer available.

Somewhere below, the Watchers were in session. They had acted once to disrupt the exchange. The exchange had happened anyway. What they would do in the next thirty-two hours — when a new machine arrived at their territory ahead of its scheduled window, before any government had been informed, before any institutional framework existed to contain what had been set in motion — was not something I could predict.

And beyond the Watchers, in a community whose full shape I had only glimpsed, there were presences I had not yet encountered and positions I had not yet heard. Sable had spoken from the Bridge. The Watchers had acted. What else existed in the deep, and what it thought, was still entirely unknown to me.

That was part of what I did not yet know how to hold.

"Chen," I said.

"On hold," Reyes said. "He's been waiting for my callback since 07.15."

"Langvik," I said.

"Your institute's communications system has been trying to reach you since the comms restored. Your department head is apparently quite urgent."

"The Bergen fire," I said. "My data."

"Yes. That's the official version of events. The investigation is already underway." He paused. "Most of your cloud backups are intact. The unrecoverable data is — recent. The last three weeks."

The exchange sessions. The preliminary framework documents. The recordings I had been making in parallel with Yuna's translation work.

"Yuna has the originals," I said.

"Yes."

"In her notebooks."

"Yes."

I thought about the Watchers and their decision to destroy what was on the Bergen servers and leave what was in Yuna's hands. Their surveillance was acoustic and passive — they knew what was in the ocean's data. They didn't know what was in a notebook.

I thought: they may have just made a mistake.

* * *

I stood at the rail for a while after Reyes went back to the communications room. The sun was fully up now — properly up, the flat northern sun giving no warmth but giving light, the Norwegian Sea resolved into its full detail: the texture of the surface, the colour of the water, the horizon precisely where it always was.

Thirty-two hours. Chen on hold. Langvik urgent. Sixteen hours of queued messages. A new rig underway. The Watchers in session somewhere below.

And us. Three people on a research vessel with no comms authority that anyone had approved, with data the institution hadn't sanctioned, with a translation framework that existed in one person's notebooks, with a conversation that no government or organisation or official body had authorised, that had happened anyway because the alternative was something neither species could afford.

And now the conversation had happened. The silence was broken in both directions. There was no version of the next thirty-two hours in which everything stayed contained. A rig was en route. The Watchers were active. Whatever institutional response was coming — from Chen, about the thirty-two hours before Aurora Eight arrived; from the Norwegian government; from whoever else had been watching the dark vessel's footage — was arriving in hours, not days.

I thought about what Reyes had said on the morning of the first descent, when I had told him I didn't think it mattered whether I was ready: *I don't think it matters. We need to go.*

I thought: we needed to go then. We need to say something now.

I thought about the word *all* in the sentence I was about to say. *All of us.* Not me and Reyes. Not the three of us on this deck. All — the governments, the institutions, the people who had been watching from the dark vessel and from the satellite feed and from behind the cover story of a maritime safety audit. The people who would find out in days or weeks regardless, when a rig arrived at a location where a sealed rig was already sitting on the bottom, when the communications blackout became public record, when Langvik's urgent calls stopped being answerable with standard institute protocols.

All of us. The whole species, eventually. All of them would have to know. The only question was the order in which they found out and what they found out first.

I looked at the water. Below it — not so far, in the scheme of things, not compared to what lived in the hadal zone — the Aurora Seven sat with its lights on and its crew alive and its hatches sealed. And below that, the structure. And beyond the structure, in the deep itself — in a community that extended across a geography I had not seen and could not yet imagine — the Hadali went about what they went about: a continuity that predated terrestrial life, briefly interrupted by the necessity of speaking to the surface.

They had come up. They had said what they came to say.

Now the surface had to do something with it.

I picked up the satellite phone Reyes had left on the equipment case.

It was warm from being in his jacket pocket.

I looked at it. I thought about Chen on hold, about Langvik urgent, about the sixteen hours of queued messages, about the thirty-two hours before Aurora Eight arrived. I thought about the fact that not one of those calls, not one of those messages, was from anyone who knew what I knew. Not yet.

I thought about all of the things I was going to have to say, and about the order I was going to say them in, and about what would happen to the saying once it entered the institutional channels that were about to receive it.

I thought about the first chapter I would have to write of whatever came next.

The phone was warm in my hand. The sun was up over the Norwegian Sea. Somewhere below, something ancient and vast and patient was back in the deep, attending, waiting to see what the listeners would do.

I pressed call.

"We need to talk," I said. "All of us."

THANK YOU FOR READING

If you've reached this page, you have spent a handful of hours in Mara's world. Thank you. For an independent author, every reader is a quiet gift, and I don't take a single one for granted.

If SIGNAL held you — or even if it didn't, and you know why — the single most useful thing you can do is leave an honest review on Amazon or Goodreads. Reviews are how indie books find their next readers. They don't need to be long. A few sentences about what worked, or didn't, makes a genuine difference.

If you'd like to tell me directly, you can reach me at **cainota.com**.

— *Cole Vane*

THE STORY CONTINUES IN

DEPTH

The negotiation. The fracture. The cost of knowing.

The secret held. The aftermath is breaking.

Coming soon

Visit cainota.com to be notified the day DEPTH is released.

Sign up for newsletter at

cainota.com

The newsletter will be quiet. I write when the next book is ready to be released. You can unsubscribe at any time, and I will never share your address.

www.ingramcontent.com/pod-product-compliance
Lightning Source LLC
LaVergne TN
LVHW090517110826
845146LV00003B/894

* 9 7 8 9 9 1 6 4 3 8 9 3 0 *